A Rock In A Hard Place

A Rock In A Hard Place

Faizah Imani

Aventine Press LLC

Published by Aventine Press, LLC
2208 Cabo Bahia
Chula Vista, CA 91914, USA

www.aventinepress.com

ISBN: 1-59330-058-1

Acknowledgements

First and foremost, I have to give all of the honor and glory to God. If it weren't for You, there would be no me. I thank You, Heavenly Father, for everything that You have blessed me to endure. All of the storms that came my way only made me stronger in You and in Your word. If I could, I wouldn't go back and change a thing. You worked it all out for my good. But most importantly, for the good of Your Kingdom. And per Your command Father, I will now go and strengthen my brethren. *Luke 22:31-32*

Thank You Jesus for dying in my stead so that I may have eternal life. If it weren't for You, I wouldn't be here doing what I am doing today---spreading the GREAT news of Jesus Christ!!!!

Thank You Holy Spirit for being my Comforter, my Teacher and my Counselor. I pray that You will continue to speak to me and through me. Oh GREAT Divine Revelator. You are welcome to abide in this temple forever. I wouldn't trade You for the world.

In the name of Jesus!!! Amen.

To Jaza, my daughter: You are a special gift from God. You mean more than the world to me. And I love you dearly.

To the Tonth family: I love you. And words can never express my gratitude for all of the guidance that you have given me along the way. Thanks for everything. You guys are truly Heaven sent. I pray that God blesses you all.

To Noel Tuazon, my cover illustrator: I know for a fact that it was not by chance that our paths crossed. You were truly God-Sent. I know I wasn't the easiest person to work with.   Because you were willing to work with me on a cover concept that was divinely revealed, I know that God is going to bless you.

To my New Hope church family: I love you. God's Spirit is alive and well at New Hope!!!

Pastor Clarke: You probably don't know me from Adam, but I thank God for sending you to be the earthly shepherd of my soul. The Spirit of the Lord is upon you. And your Divinely inspired messages have helped me in more ways than you can ever imagine. I feel like I can conquer the world. I pray that God continues to annoint you, to use you, and to bless you and your beautiful family tremendously...

Last, but not least, thanks to all of my Teletech associates who have supported me and given we words of encouragement along the way...William, Tequila, Sarathia and all the rest of you.

If I left off anyone's name, charge it to my mind and not my heart. I love you all and I pray that God blesses you all!!!

Chapter One

As I sit here staring out the window of this Washington D.C bound airplane, I am officially declaring myself to be under a Rock in a hard place. How did I get here? Child, it's a long story. But if you'll sit down for a minute, I'll try to explain as much as I can.

By the way, my name is Daija.

Allow me to rewind the tape of my life back to the very beginning. I am only 20 years old, so you would think that the tape of my life wouldn't have very much rewinding to do. I wish that were true. But it's not. Tons of heartache and pain have been felt during these 20 years. Thank God I made it through.

It all started in a small town called Vardaman, Mississippi. Unbeknownst to many as the "sweet potato capital of the world." (Actually, Vardaman was more like a village than a town. The population couldn't be more than five hundred.)

My mom, whose name was Tisa, almost died when I was born. Now in most cases, a situation such as this would form a bond between a mother and child. Well, in my case it didn't.

A few days after Tisa brought me home from the hospital, she decided to go AWOL, or better yet AWOD. Absent without Daija. As a result, I was raised by Tisa's' mom, also known as Grandma Ginetta.

Grandma Ginetta was what some people would call a dimepiece because of her good looks. Looks that I am grateful to have inherited. A fox she was, with silky straight salt and pepper hair that was so long she could tie it under her chin in a knot two times. She always wore it pinned up in a neat little bun on the back of her head. It was her "teacher" look. And although she's retired from that profession, she still maintained it.

She had successfully raised two children in a single parent home. But her honey-coated complexion didn't have a wrinkle to show for it. She never revealed her age to anyone. However, if I had to guestimate, I would say that she was in her mid-fifties.

My Grandma was a very laid back, religious lady. And although she was somewhat old fashioned, she instilled in me high moral values and Christian ethics. She always taught me to be proud of who I am. And that although I wasn't the richest kid on the block, I was just as good as they were. That I should never feel inferior to anyone because God made us all equal. She was full of wisdom. And could probably give King Solomon a run for his money.

The only bad thing grandma had going for her was that she had a long list of health problems. Everything ranging from heart problems to diabetes.

The heart problems were mostly due to all of the heartache and pain that Tisa had caused. But despite how bad my grandma's health was, she never abandoned me.

Grandma Ginetta never talked much about my mom. And she made it a point not to say anything negative about her in my presence.

She tried to be secretive about the details of how she got stuck raising me. However, being that Vardaman was so small, everybody knew each other. And as a result, everybody also knew everybody's business. After years and years of listening to the gossip around town, I managed to draw my own conclusion as to what happened.

Gossip folks say that Tisa left when I was only a few weeks old. She supposedly went to get her hair done at the beauty shop one rainy afternoon and she never came back. Folks around town thought she had been kidnapped or something. Until she finally managed to call Grandma Ginetta to let her know that she was in Georgia—with my potential daddy.

I never received confirmation from Grandma Ginetta whether or not this is what really happened. But the stories that I have managed to hear through the years have remained pretty consistent.

I don't remember ever spending any time with Tisa. But Grandma swore up and down that she came to visit me twice after she disappeared. Aunt Tee-Ona, Grandma's oldest child who lives in Chicago, was the only person that Tisa kept in contact with on a semi-regular basis. And that was probably due to the fact that she had a lot of money.

One Saturday morning, Grandma received a telephone call while I was sitting on the living room floor watching cartoons and playing with my baby dolls. It was Tisa. The only time that Tisa called on a non-birthday or a non-holiday was when she wanted something. And this time was no different. It turns out that she wanted to know if she could come back and live with us, because she was pregnant again and had just lost her job. She had eight months left to go before the baby was due.

Of course, being the caring person that Grandma Ginetta was, she told Tisa that she could come back to live. But there was a condition attached. The condition was that my mom had to agree to start taking responsibility for her actions. Get a job. And raise her own kids.

Being that Grandma was a retired teacher, she didn't have a ton of money. The little money she did have was mainly spent on taking care of a child that wasn't hers. And although I was only seven years old, I knew deep down in my heart that it bothered her.

Shockingly, Tisa agreed to come home and take care of me and my, soon to be, sibling.

For some bizarre reason, I became anxious to have my mom come stay with us. My imagination ran wild with visions of us playing games like dress up, reading bedtime stories, and doing all of the other little fun things that mothers and daughters supposedly do. That was my intended itinerary. I was so excited that I was finally going to be able to meet my mom. I could hardly wait.

A few days had passed since the telephone conversation had transpired between Grandma Ginetta and my mom. Everyday, after I got home from school and did my homework, I would rush to the door, sit down and stare at it with hopes that my real mom would eventually come walking through.

Days turned into weeks and weeks turned into months. Still no Tisa.

I assumed that Grandma would tell me if Tisa had decided not to come. However, that is an assumption that was made in error. Can't say that I blame her. I'm sure it's hard to look a child in the eyes and tell them that the one thing they are hoping for will never be manifested. One day it finally dawned on me that Tisa wasn't coming.

It took me a while to get over my disappointment. But I managed. People cope with disappointment in different ways. I coped with mine by pretending that the situation didn't exist. I pretended that Tisa didn't exist. She became a mere figment of my imagination—until that day. A day that she quickly became a reality.

Chapter Two

A few months after I had recuperated from my disappointment, a lady showed up at our door with a newborn baby boy. I could see her through the glass window that was on the side of our living room door.

She was carrying the baby in, what looked like, a picnic basket. And she was wearing very shabby clothes--like those bad women that grandma say be standing on the street corner asking men for money. Her makeup was heavily applied and she had long red hair. I had never seen the lady a day in my life. But despite how weird she looked, there was something peculiar about her. I couldn't put my finger on it.

Grandma always told me not to open the door for strangers, so I ran into the kitchen to let her know that a strange looking lady was at the door carrying a baby. She looked at me as if she had seen a ghost. Immediately dropping everything that she was doing, she ran into the living room, leaving a flour trail on the freshly vacuumed carpet.

To my surprise, she opened the door for the lady without asking who she was nor what she wanted.

Once the lady stepped inside, the only words (or should I say WORD) that she and Grandma Ginetta exchanged was a very nonchalant "Hi."

One of Grandma Ginetta's old-fashioned rules was that when grown folks are around, children should disappear. So I knew something was very wrong when she went back into the kitchen and left me in the living room to entertain our guest.

In the meantime, the lady was still standing there in the middle of the living room floor with the baby basket in her hands. I wanted to ask her if I had a bugar in my nose--because why else would she be staring at me like that. Grandma Ginetta always told me not to be sassy with grown folks. So rather than say anything, I gazed down at the floor and pretended to be ignorant of the fact that she was still staring.

I was silently thinking to myself, "Why did grandma leave me in the room with this strange lady?"

All of a sudden, I had this urge to go pee. I always have to pee when I get nervous. I decided to get up and go to the bathroom because the urge had become overwhelming.

Just as I was getting ready to make a run for the bathroom, grandma came out of the kitchen and sat down on the living room sofa. The lady was still standing up as if she was getting ready to turn around and walk back out the door.

"Are you in such a hurry that you can't sit down and say hello to your daughter?"

What is Grandma Ginetta talking about? What daughter? I didn't understand.

The lady finally sat down the picnic basket with the baby in it and kneeled down in front of me.

She dropped her head and paused for a brief moment, as if she was thinking about something. When she looked up, we were eye level to one another. She then spoke her first words to me since she had entered our house. They were words that I will remember for as long as I live.

"Daija." She paused again and took a deep sigh. "I am your mother."

I turned around to look at Grandma Ginetta. Her eyes were filled with tears.

I turned back around to face the lady again.

I was trying with all my might to fight back the tears.

My voice started to crack. "You're---my mom?"

I couldn't believe that my mom was actually kneeling here in front of me. The emotions that I felt at that moment could not be described with words. I felt happy. But at the same time, I felt sad. I also felt angry with her for leaving me.

All of the past disappointments came back to surface. Although I thought I wanted her to be in my life, I was mad at her for coming back. I had spent seven years of my life without her and I definitely didn't need her now.

I mean, who does she think she is, waltzing in here and telling me that she is my mother? She obviously doesn't know the meaning of the word. I may have only been seven, but I knew that there was a difference between a mother and a mama. Anybody can be a mama. But it takes someone special to be a mother. Someone special like my Grandma Ginetta. She had been all the mother I needed.

"Can I call you Tisa?" I asked.

She didn't respond. She simply dropped her head again and stared at the floor.

At that point, Grandma Ginetta intervened. "So, how long are you staying Tisa?"

She told grandma that she was only staying for a couple of days and would then be heading back to Georgia so that she could return to work.

"Are you gonna take your baby with you?" asked grandma.

"Mom, I need a favor."

It turns out that she only came into town to see if grandma could keep my baby brother for a month. She was getting ready to go back to work and needed some time to hire a babysitter for him.

"Now Tisa, I done told you that I am not taking care of any more of your babies. You should have thought about the fact that you didn't have a babysitter before you spread your---"

"You know what mom. I didn't come to argue. All I want to know is whether or not you are willing to keep Ty for a while. That's a simple yes or no question."

I couldn't believe what I was hearing. Was it really that simple for her?

"Well," grandma replied, "if it only requires a simple yes or no, then, your answer is no. I done worked my whole life just to raise my own two kids and now that I have taken care of my responsibilities, you want me to take care of yours? You stuck me with Daija. And I let you get away with that. But, I refuse Tisa. I refuse to keep any more of your kids. Maybe you need to try getting a job that won't leave you knocked up and you wouldn't have this problem."

Tisa jumped up light a bolt of lightening had struck her. She grabbed the baby basket. "You know what mama, I should've known better than to ask you for help."

She told Grandma Ginetta that if the answer was no, then she was going to take me back with her too.

"Daija, go pack your things, you are coming with me," she yelled.

Grandma started crying. "Tisa, you can't take that girl away from me, she's all I have. I have raised her and been there for her when you were nowhere to be found. Hell, taking her with you would be like kidnapping the poor child. Ten minutes ago, she didn't even know who you were. You can be mad at me all you want, but please don't take it out on Daija."

Apparently, Tisa wasn't interested in what Grandma Ginetta had to say because she kept insisting that I hurry up and pack so she could go.

"Think, Daija, think," I am saying to myself.

Grandma always told me not to sass grown folk, but I have to speak up for myself. I have got to find a way to let Tisa know that I don't want to go with her. The best thing that could happen would be that Tisa would decide not to take me with her because she'll know how much I resent her for walking out of my life. The worst thing that could happen is that grandma would give me the whipping of my life for sassing Tisa. A whipping will only sting for a few minutes. If I don't speak up, the pain is gonna sting for a lifetime.

Alright, enough contemplating. I am gonna do it. Just as I made up my mind to stand up to Tisa, she yelled at me again to go pack my things.

"No," I screamed. "I'm not going!"

"What do you mean-- you're not going?" asked Tisa. "You will do exactly what I tell you to little girl."

When she said that, it really struck a nerve that I didn't even know existed. How dare she come in here barking orders at me like that and disrespecting Grandma Ginetta. I am not going anywhere with her. I told her that I wasn't going and I meant it. I don't know exactly where all of this newfound courage came from, but I refused to back down. If I get a whipping for standing up to Tisa, I am going to earn it. It will be a well-deserved one because I am going to do whatever I have to do to keep from going with her. After all, there isn't a lot that Grandma Ginetta can do on this one because legally Tisa can take me with her. And there isn't a thing anyone can do to stop her.

By now, Grandma Ginetta had started crying uncontrollably and pleading with Tisa to not take me away from her. This scared me because Grandma has a bad heart. She can easily have a heart attack if she gets too upset. Seeing grandma upset like that just did something to me. I felt my face getting hot. I held my arms stiffly down by my side and clutched my fists really tight. I could feel something wet starting to trickle down my legs but I wasn't about to let my nervousness get the best of me. I closed my eyes really tight and all of a sudden I became the epitome of rage.

At this moment, only God can tell you the words that came out of my mouth. It's like I changed into this person that had been hiding inside of me waiting to get out. And when she finally got out, she couldn't control all of the bottled up feelings and emotions that had been suppressed for seven years.

I felt as if my heart was an erupting volcano---and the words that were spewing out of my mouth were like molten hot lava. Burning everything in sight. When I was done erupting, I felt liberated.

It took a few seconds for me to snap out of my rage. When I finally did, I honestly thought grandma was gonna kill me. I don't know what I had said to Tisa, but by the look that was on Grandma Ginetta's face, it was a mouthful. Grandma didn't say anything. She was speechless and so was I.

Tisa looked at Grandma Ginetta. "This is all your fault," she said. "All you do is sit around here and put bad thoughts in her head about me."

"You stop talking to my grandma like that. She don't talk about you at all, much less put thoughts in my head about you. I put my own thoughts in my head about you. And the way I feel about you is your fault, not Grandma's."

"Well," said Tisa, "on that note, I guess it's time for me to go."

"I guess it is," I was silently thinking. I didn't say it out loud because I figured that I had already said enough to get a whipping that would last ten lifetimes. I guess when nobody said anything back to her, she got the hint. She picked up the baby basket and walked out the door. And just like that, she was gone again.

I looked at grandma. She didn't say anything, but she and I had this silent communication thing going. I could tell from the look on her face that she was proud of me for making the decision not to go with Tisa. She still had tears in her eyes. And I felt compelled to walk over and give her a big hug. So I did. Then I remembered that I had to go change clothes because in the midst of my rage I had peed on myself.

I was heading to my room to change, when suddenly, I heard a baby crying. My heart started racing a thousand times a minute as I ran back to look out of the living room window. What if my mom had decided to take me with her regardless of how I felt?

When I looked out of the window, I didn't see Tisa anywhere. I guess the crying baby was just a figment of my imagination. I went on to my room. Changed my clothes. And came back to join grandma who was still on the living room sofa.

Our living room furniture had to have been every bit of fifty years old. Although it was all worn and torn, grandma still had the plastic cover on it. Normally, I would sit on the floor. It was more comfortable than sitting on the furniture. The plastic made my bottom sweat. But, I guess because of everything that had just happened, I really felt like sitting next to my grandma. So I went and sat down on the sofa beside her and turned on the TV.

It was time for Sesame Street to come on. That was one of the few non-cartoon shows that I watched religiously. After Sesame Street had been on for a couple of minutes, I suddenly heard a baby crying again. Apparently, this time Grandma Ginetta heard it too.

She went and opened the door to see where the crying was coming from. When she opened the door, she discovered that Tisa had left her a package on the way out. It was my baby brother, Ty.

Chapter
Three

I am now thirteen years old and my little brother Ty is six. Although times were hard before Ty came into the picture, they seem a breeze compared to the way things are now.

Despite the way that Tisa left my little brother with us, Grandma Ginetta and I both felt that she would eventually come back after she found a baby-sitter. However, six years had passed. And it didn't take a rocket scientist to finally realize that she wasn't coming back.

Getting full around our house had suddenly become a luxury. Food was always scarce and money was always tight. Grandma Ginetta's health had deteriorated. And the doctors had upped her dosage of heart medications. Which meant more money spent on medicine and less money spent on house necessities--such as food.

The irony is that despite how detrimental grandma's high salt and pork diet was to the rapid deterioration of her health, she refused to give it up. Or maybe she just couldn't afford to give it up. Pork was cheap. And she could get a lot of it for very little money. Some people would call it "the poor man's meat."

We relied a lot nowadays on Aunt Tee-Ona, Grandma Ginetta's oldest child. She had to send us money every month just for us to make it through. Grandma hated having to take money from Aunt Tee-Ona. So she eventually went out and got a part time job in the evenings sitting with an elderly lady just to try and make ends meet. The ends still didn't meet. As a matter of fact, I think the ends hated each other because they never came close to meeting.

I was now old enough to go out and do little odd and end jobs to try and help out around the house. In the summertime, I would go door to door mowing lawns for ten dollars a yard. In the fall, I would rake leaves for ten dollars a yard. Sometimes in the spring, Grandma Ginetta would have a few friends that needed help with their spring-cleaning. I hated cleaning our own house much less someone else's. But somehow grandma always managed to volunteer me to help her friends out. She said that we needed the money. And besides I never questioned grandma. When she told us to do something, we knew not to hesitate.

In a way, I also felt obligated to do whatever I could to bring money into the house. Most of the time all I can think about is how Grandma Ginetta is probably feeling on the inside knowing that she has struggled and worked so hard for twenty five years, only to retire and not have anything to show for it.

I stayed so busy trying to help out around the house that I didn't really have a whole lot of free time on my hands. After school let out, I would always rush home to take care of Ty while Grandma Ginetta went to work.

It didn't bother me much to have to baby-sit my little brother because it allowed me and Ty to form a really good brother and sister type of bond. I didn't have many friends so I ended up telling most of my problems to a six-year-old who had no earthly idea what I was talking about.

It was difficult being in the seventh grade. I was always afraid that the other kids would discover how poor my family was. Most of my peers participated in band or choir. They would always ask me why I wasn't participating, but my excuse was always the same--"I didn't have time." None of them knew how poor we were and that the real reason I wasn't participating was because I knew grandma couldn't afford it.

I had always dreamed of being in the band every since I can remember. It's just something about going to the parades and seeing them marching down the streets in their pretty uniforms with the fluffy feathers on their hats and big shiny instruments.

I remember how bad Grandma Ginetta felt when I had to drop my piano class. For that reason, I never asked her if I could participate in any of the activities at school because I didn't want her to feel bad about not being able to afford it. I pretended that it didn't matter.

Chapter Four

My best friend's name was Angela. She lived around the corner from us and we had been friends since first grade. Like the majority of my peers, she was also in the band. She played the clarinet. But she also had a trombone that she no longer used.

Whenever I went to visit Angela, we would march around the house parading and pretending that we were in a two-man band. It's probably the closest I'll ever get to being in a band. For that reason, I savored every minute of it.

Angela's mom was a big time lawyer and her father was a doctor. They had everything that a person could ever dream of wanting. Her parents had always wanted a second child but were unable to have another one. In their own little way, they adopted me into their family as a second child. They knew that my family didn't have much. And they always offered to help us in anyway they possibly could. But Grandma Ginetta wasn't one to quickly take handouts from other people, and therefore we never took them up on their offer.

As hard as I tried to be ignorantly unaware of the things that we didn't have, somehow, being around Angela and her family forced me to acknowledge just how poor my family was.

Although I never mentioned it to anyone, Angela's parents knew how much I wanted to be in the band. I guess they could tell because of how excited I always got when I played around with Angela's instruments.

One day, while I was over visiting, they told me that if grandma didn't object to me being in the band, they would allow me to use Angela's Trombone since she was no longer using it.

I couldn't believe my ears! I finally had the opportunity to be in the band. I was so sure that grandma wouldn't object to it because she had always wanted me to be able to participate in some of the activities at school that we couldn't afford. It's not that band was all that expensive. But you do have to buy your own instrument. Now that I have free access to an instrument, I have no excuses. I couldn't wait to run home and tell Grandma Ginetta the news.

I was so anxious and excited about the opportunity that had been presented before me that I skipped the entire way home. As soon as I got there, I told Grandma Ginetta the news. She was a little more hesitant than I had expected her to be. I am sure that it was because of her extensive pride. Grandma didn't like taking handouts from anybody. Regardless of the reason. She did say that she would give it some consideration though. So at least there was a little bit of hope left. But for some reason, I wasn't as enthusiastic about the idea of being in band anymore. I think it was because of the cold response I had received from Grandma Ginetta. Seems like everytime I get my hopes up for something, I end up getting disappointed.

The more I tried to pretend that I didn't care about what grandma's final decision would be--the more anxious I became. When I saw Angela the next day at school, she mentioned that Grandma Ginetta had called to their house last night asking to speak with her parents. Although Angela wasn't sure about the extent of their conversation, she did say that she overheard her mom mention me being in the band.

Hearing this news made me feel a little bit better. At least I knew that grandma was giving it some consideration.

After school, I decided to stop by the band room with Angela and meet the band director, Mr. Davenport. Most of the girls at school were crazy about him. Some even had secret crushes. There were no guarantees that I was going to be in the band but there's no harm in meeting the man.

When I walked into the band room, I felt as if I had died and gone to heaven. Huge, shiny, brass instruments were hanging on the walls and there were instrument cases all over the place. Angela pointed to Mr. Davenport's office. I could actually see him talking on the phone.

Some of the kids were sitting in their chairs practicing and others were just standing around talking to one another. They appeared to be having so much fun mingling around in the band room.

"Hey you guys," yelled Angela to get everyone's attention, "This is my friend Daija, and she's gonna be joining the band."

I was completely embarrassed. I have never been one to like a lot of attention and now it seems as if all eyes were on me.

"Hi Daija," everyone yelled, almost in unison while giving me a round of applause.

I could actually feel myself blushing. I had never gotten that much attention from any of my peers at school. And it made me feel all warm and fuzzy on the inside. I felt as if I actually fit in.

Apparently, Mr. Davenport heard all of the commotion because he stepped out of his office, "What's going on in here?"

One of the kids yelled out, "Hey Mr. D, we were just welcoming Daija! She's gonna be joining the band!"

"Is that right?" asked Mr. Davenport as he turned to look at me.

Now I was really blushing. When he looked at me, I could see why the girls at school were so crazy about him. The man was fine.

In awe of his beauty, I managed to squeak out a reply, "Yes, ummmmm-----Mr. Davenport. That is, if you don't mind----sir."

"Well then, I guess we need to have a talk," said Mr. Davenport, smiling.

His smile was so warming. "Step into my office," he said as he started walking away.

I looked at Angela. She had a devilish grin on her face as she motioned for me to go ahead. I followed Mr. Davenport into his office.

He had a lot of plaques and awards on his wall. There were also some pictures hanging around of him and the band. I got the impression that this man really loved his job.

I was somewhat nervous and had the urge to go to the restroom but I managed to hold it in.

"So, you want to be in my band?" asked Mr. Davenport, as he reclined back in his chair and propped his feet up on top of his desk.

"Yes, sir."

"Why do you want to be in my band?"

I was trying to think of a good answer, but I couldn't. So, I just told him how I have always enjoyed the parades and how I liked the uniforms and big shiny instruments. Blah, blah, blah...

"Well, you do know that there is a lot more to the band than the pretty uniforms and big shiny instruments don't you?"

"What do you mean sir?"

"Being in the band requires a whole lot of dedication and hard work," replied Mr. Davenport, "Do you have it to give?"

"Actually sir, there is no guarantee that I will be in the band. My grandma hasn't decided whether or not she is going to allow me to participate. I just came to the band room today with my friend Angela. She was the one who announced to everyone that I was going to be joining the band."

"I see," said Mr. Davenport. "Well, if you have the time to give and are willing to put in the necessary hardwork that it takes to be a part of this band, then I'll be glad to have you. And if there is anything that I can say to your grandma to convince her to allow you to participate with us then be sure to let me know."

" Will do, sir." I replied.

He stood up and extended his hand for a handshake. "If your grandma decides to let you join us, then you be sure to stop back by my office so that we can talk about some things that it is very imperative that you know."

"Will do, Mr. Davenport." I replied as I shook his hand.

"Please---call me Mr. D." he insisted.

I felt like fainting. The man had charisma out of this world.

"Ok then. Mr. D it is." I replied blushingly.

He and I left out of the office at the same time. Angela was packing up her instrument. She drilled me the entire way home about what Mr. Davenport and I talked about and was eager to know every single detail. What did he say? How did he say it? How was he looking when he said it? I mean the girl was obsessed with the man. I do have to admit though that he was quite a cutie.

When I got home from school, grandma was finishing up dinner. Pork---as usual. And Ty was in the living room watching cartoons.

Any other time, I would have fought with him to get control of the TV, but I decided to let him have it. I wanted to stay in Grandma Ginetta's good graces so that, hopefully, she would render a favorable decision regarding my participation in the band. I would have volunteered to clean the house, however, being that grandma didn't have to work today, she had already completed all of the household chores. I decided to go to my room and get my homework done while grandma finished up dinner.

It took me about forty five minutes to complete homework that normally would have only taken me fifteen minutes to finish. My anxiety was getting the best of me. So I found it difficult to concentrate.

"Daija, it's time for dinner!" grandma yelled in the background.

I darted out of my room and fell flat on my back as soon as I opened the door. Ty was sitting at the end of the hallway laughing. The little evil twerp had inten-tionally placed all of his marbles outside my bedroom door and was waiting for me to come out and trip over them. Before I knew it, I was charging after him like a raging bull and had he not ran in the kitchen and hid behind Grandma Ginetta he was about to get one right in the mouth.

"Grandma, grandma, Daija trying to hit me!!!

"Was not!" I yelled.

"Were too!"

"Alright enough from the two of you. We are going to sit down and have a peaceful dinner for once," said grandma.

Ty stuck his tongue out at me. I felt like I was breathing fire right now, I was so hot and mad at him. It's amazing how that boy works my nerves. What's even more amazing is how he went from being my small, adorable baby brother to being the devil's son-in-law. I'll get him back though if it's the last thing I do.

It was hard for me to enjoy my dinner because I was still pissed off at Ty.

"Daija, I have given a lot of thought and consideration into what you asked me about the band," said grandma.

I sat straight up in my chair at attention. "Yes--- grandma," I said eagerly.

She continued, "I've also spoken with Angela's parents about their proposal of allowing you to use Angela's band instrument."

"Yes--grandma," I replied even more eagerly than before.

"Well, you have always done really well in school. You always do whatever you can to help out around here and I really appreciate that. You never ask for anything. And I hate that I can't afford to give you a lot of the things that some of your friends may have. But it's hard when you are living on a fixed income. It was very generous of Angela's parents to be willing to let you use their daughter's instrument. Unfortunately, having an instrument is just a small part of being in the band. It takes money. Money that we don't have."

"That's alright grandma. I understand." I managed to whisper.

I tried to hide the disappointment in my voice. I could feel a lump rising in my throat and tears starting to well up in my eyes. I knew where this conversation was going.

Of course, Ty had to interject his two cents. "Neh neh neh neh neh, you can't be in the band!"

I was too hurt right now to be mad at him. "I'm not hungry anymore. May I be dismissed?" I asked grandma.

"Wait a minute little lady, I'm not finished yet. As I was saying. I hate that I can't give you a lot of the things your friends might have. I know how bad you want to be in the band. I simply can't afford it---by myself, that is. However, Angela's parents are willing to help out in any way that they can. So, I have decided to let you be in the band."

Oh my goodness! Did I just hear what I thought I heard? "Are you saying that I can be in the band?"

"Yes, Daija, you can be in the band," grandma replied as she laughed at my excitement.

"Oh Grandma!" I jumped up and gave her a big hug and kiss on the cheek.

"You deserve it dear," she said with a smile.

I started doing a little dance as I poked fun at Ty. "Neh neh neh neh neh, I'm gonna be in the band."

I would have called Angela to tell her the news, but it was after eight o' clock. She wasn't allowed to receive calls after eight on school nights. So I would have to wait and tell her at school tomorrow. I could hardly wait.

Chapter
Five

It's funny how time flies when you're having fun. I have been in the band for going on four years now. And if I wasn't falling asleep with my head in my books, I was falling asleep with my band instrument by my side. Band had slowly become my outlet. And Mr. Davenport had become a huge father figure to me.

Although, I auditioned for every solo competition that arose, made every all-city and every all-state band, he was always pushing me and encouraging me to do better. To try harder and to never become complacent when it came to the talents that God has blessed me with. He was the only male figure I had. And I really looked up to him.

As I entered my senior year in high school, I was elected band president and president of the national honors society. While my peers were still trying to decide whether or not they wanted to apply for college, I had already applied and gotten accepted into Howard University. I was offered several scholarships from various other schools. But grandma wanted me to choose Howard. She said that it was an excellent school that had a lot of notoriety.

Angela had also gotten accepted into Howard. Although, I don't exactly know how because her grades were less than perfect. Her parents were both Howard Alumni. Rumor has it that they paid the admissions counselor a lump sum of money to admit their daughter into the university. As far as I was concerned, it didn't matter. I was just happy that my best friend and I were going off to college together.

Ty had mellowed out a whole lot. He didn't get on my nerves as much anymore. And he had stopped playing the "put marbles outside of your sisters door and sit there and watch her fall" games. For once, we were actually getting along like siblings. Of course we had our spats every now and then, but nothing more than what any other brother and sister had.

For the first time in my life, everything felt perfect. Our financial stature had not changed much. But I was never the type to let our money problems get me down anyway. You can't miss what you can't measure. Just as I began to think that things couldn't get any better---things got worse.

I came home from school one day and Grandma Ginetta was sitting on the living room sofa singing and swaying to her gospel music. Instead of just saying hello--why didn't I just sit down and have a quality conversation with her for once? Tell her how much I love her. How much I appreciate her.

Instead of spending quality time with grandma, I proceeded to do my daily chores as usual. . When I finished, I went on to my room so that I could complete my homework.

After I had been in my room a few minutes, I heard grandma yelling, "Daija, turn the air on baby. It's getting hot in here!"

"Ok grandma!"

I waited a couple of minutes though because I was working on a hard math equation and didn't want to lose my train of thought.

I finally got up and and hit the thermostat in the hallway to turn the air on. After I turned it on, I noticed that grandma had gotten awfully quiet. I went into the living room and she had her head down. I had this feeling that she wasn't saying a prayer.

"Grandma."

She didn't answer me.

"Grandma, are you ok?"

Still no answer.

I was trying not to panic but I couldn't help it. I ran over to her and shook her, "Grandma!" "Grandma wake up!"

She didn't budge.

I put my finger under her nose to see if I felt any air coming out. There was air coming out so I knew she was alive. I kept shaking her but she wouldn't wake up.

We didn't have a telephone anymore. So, at this point my panicking had gotten out of control.

"I need to call 911! I have to get someone to call 911!" The tears wouldn't stop flowing.

"Grandma wake up!"

I tried giving CPR. But I was so emotional I wasn't sure if I was doing it right. "I gotta get some help!"

I ran out of the house and started screaming. Hoping that anyone would hear my cry for help. I ran down the street and stopped at the first house I got to. After bamming on the door for about a minute, a little old lady finally opened it. I could hardly breathe and I felt like I was having an anxiety attack.

"Please help me! Please! call 911!!! My grandma. She won't wake up! She needs help! We--need help!"

The lady let me in to use the phone. I made it quick. The 911 dispatcher wanted to hold a conversation with me but I didn't have time. I told her the problem and gave her the address and slammed down the phone.

"Thank you!" I cried as I ran out the door and back home.

Grandma Ginetta was still out cold. She was still breathing though. I just sat there and cried as I held her and rocked her in my arms. "It's gonna be alright grandma. You hang in there. You're going to be alright! Please God. Don't let my grandma die!"

Finally after about 10 minutes of waiting, the ambulance showed up. I opened the door and they almost knocked me down trying to get in with their medical equipment.

The paramedics took her off of the sofa and laid her on the floor. They attempted CPR and it wasn't working. They cut her dress off and tried the shock treatment. That didn't work either.

"We gotta get her to the hospital." one of the workers stated. He turned to face me, "Are you the only one here?"

"Yes-sir. My little brother is at his friends house."

"We're gonna have to take her to the hospital." he stated as they put her on the stretcher. "We're gonna need someone to sign her in."

"I'm going with her. Grandma Ginetta needs me."

I taped a note outside the door informing Ty that we had to rush grandma to the hospital.

They wouldn't let me ride in the back of the ambulance with her. They were still working on her and I would only be in the way. So I rode up front with the driver.

When we got to the hospital, they didn't waste any time getting her out of the ambulance and into the building. They whisked her away so fast, I didn't even see which way they went.

The ambulance driver apparently noticed how emotional I was and patted me on the back. "It's gonna be ok kid."

"Is she going to be alright?" I asked.

"The doctors are going to do everything in their power to save your grandmother. Just stay strong. It's gonna be alright. And just know that God will never put anything on you that you can't handle."

I didn't really understand why he said the last part but I thanked him for the words of encouragement.

I went to the front desk to check grandma into the hospital. Most of the questions they asked me, I didn't know the answer to. But I tried. After I checked her in, the receptionist took me into a room by myself. There was a television and a telephone.

"We have reserved this room for you and any other family members that might show up."

"Is my grandma going to be alright?" I asked the receptionist, with tears in my eyes.

"The doctors are working with your grandma right now as best they can sweetheart. It appears that she may have had a heart attack. As soon as we get any updates on her condition, we'll let you know. Feel free to use the telephone. Long distance calls are free but we ask that you limit long distance calls to three minutes. If you need anything, I'll be at the front desk."

After the receptionist left the room, I just put my face in my hands and cried. This can't be happening. This is all a bad dream. I'm going to wake up and everything is going to be back to normal.

A couple of hours ago, I was having the perfect day. And now. Hours later. I am having the perfect nightmare."

I tried to pull myself together so that I could call Aunt Tee-Ona and let her know what had happened. As soon as she answered the phone, I got all choked up.

"It's Grandma."

"What's wrong Daija--What's going on?"

"Grandma had to be rushed to the hospital. They think she had a heart attack."

I went on to inform her of everything that had happened, including the fact that I didn't know where Ty was.

Before I could finish, Aunt Tee-Ona cut me off, "I'm on the next flight out of here. I'll call to check on you when I get on the plane."

I didn't think I could make it through another telephone call, so I didn't call anybody else. I sat back down on the chair and starting rewinding the events that had taken place today.

After I had been in the room for about an hour, a man dressed as a priest walked in. My heart starting pounding as I jumped to my feet. "How's my grandma?"

"The doctors are still working with her."

"Have there been any improvements?"

"I'm afraid not." He replied. "I am the hospital chaplain. I just wanted to step in and offer you some words of consolation."

"I don't need any consolation. I want to know how my grandmother is doing. Can I go see her?"

"I think it would be best if you waited in the waiting area while the doctors continue working with her.   Are you here alone?" he asked me.

"Yes Sir."

"Well, you are a mighty brave young lady."

Just as he said that, the door opened again.

This time it was the doctors. "Are you the party that's here with Ginetta Rogers?"

The chaplain eased over beside me and put his hand on my shoulders. "Yes--I am." I responded.

"We are the doctors that were working with Ms. Rogers."

"What do you mean—WERE working?"

They dropped their heads. "We tried everything we could to save her. But we weren't able to bring her back. We regret to inform you that she didn't make it. She was officially pronounced dead about five minutes ago."

My knees buckled and I fell to the floor. I'm sure the entire hospital heard my screaming and tantrums.

The doctors told me that they had put Grandma Ginetta in a room by herself and that whenever I was prepared to do so, I could go and take a look at her body. With their heads still hung, they left the room. The chaplain stayed and tried to console me but it wasn't working. Before I knew it, I had blacked out.

When I finally came to back to my senses, the chaplain informed me that Aunt Tee-Ona had called and they had given her the news. She was already on the plane and should be here in about five hours.

Still an emotional wreck, I asked the chaplain to show me to Grandma Ginetta's room.

They had Grandma's white sheet covered body lying on a table. The tears of unbelief that were flowing like a river ---started flowing like an ocean as I eased over to the table beside her. I slowly pulled the sheet back. And that's when reality really sunk in that my Grandma was gone.

I kissed her forehead and brushed her hair back with my hands. All I could do was stand there and hold her hand in mine. Her fingernails were still rubyred from the manicure I had given her two days ago.

Scene after scene of the times that we had shared together kept flashing before my eyes. I had to get out of that room and get some fresh air because I started feeling faint again.

I sat outside the front entrance of the hospital for a couple of hours. While I was sitting outside, Ty walked up to me. He had gotten one of his friend's parents to drop him off at the hospital after reading my note.

I could see the hurt in his eyes after I told him all of the details of what had happened. He didn't want to go inside and view grandma's body right now. I think it was all too much for him to process at one time. He cried a little bit, but Ty had gotten to the stage now that he would always try to be the strong one whenever someone needed support. Now we had to support each other because it was just the two of us.

After sitting outside for another hour or so, we finally decided to go back into the hospital.

I looked at Ty, "I have to see her again. You want to come with me?"

He nodded his head in agreement.

I just wanted to be near her. We only stayed long enough for me to kiss her forehead again. Ty did the same. When he kissed her cold forehead he finally broke down. We went back into the family waiting room and stayed there until Aunt Tee-Ona arrived.

I could tell she had been crying. She hugged me and Ty, "Are you two alright?" she asked.

We nodded our heads.

She went in to view grandma's body for a few minutes while me and Ty stayed in the waiting room. When she came out, she was wiping away the tears with her handkerchief. "Where are the doctors?" she asked.

"I haven't seen them since they told me that grandma had passed. Ask the receptionist. She should know."

"Alright. You two stay right here. After I talk with the doctors, we are going to the house."

"Ok Aunt Tee."

On the way home Aunt Tee-Ona told me that the doctors had informed her that grandma had been prescribed some nitro-glycerin pills that were supposed to be put under her tongue in the case of a heart attack. She wanted to know if I had given her one of the pills.

My voice started cracking, "I didn't know she had them Aunt Tee." The tears came to surface again.

It's ok Daija. You didn't know."

"No. It's not Ok. Maybe if I had just given her one of those pills. This would have never happened. Grandma would still be here."

"I don't want you thinking like that Daija. There was nothing that you or anyone else could have done. It was just her time to go."

The rest of the way home, we were in complete silence. The guilt was starting to eat me up inside after hearing that one pill could have saved grandma's life.

We walked in the house to discover grandma's dress that had been cut off of her body still lying on the floor. Her glasses that had fallen off of her face were still lying on the sofa.

I picked up the dress and discovered that it still had Grandma Ginetta's scent on it. Closing my eyes, I held the dress up to my nose and tried to pretend that she was still here. I could smell her. But I couldn't touch her. I put her dress in a brown paper bag for safekeeping. I also noticed that her glasses still had her fingerprints on them. I picked them up and put them in the bag along with the dress. After sitting down on the sofa, I tried to come to terms with everything that had happened today.

A lot of "what ifs" kept going through my mind. Like what if I had known to give grandma that pill. Would she still be here? What if I had gotten up to turn on the air conditioner sooner than I did? Would it have made a difference? Mentally, I was beating myself up pretty bad.

Chapter Six

Aunt Tee-Ona's son, Deaven, and her husband Uncle Willie were among the family members that arrived the next day. Some of the family members were sitting in the living room socializing and recalling the fun memories they had of Grandma Ginetta. While the others, including Aunt Tee-Ona, sat at the kitchen table discussing the funeral arrangements.

Finally, the person that I dreaded seeing the most showed up. I couldn't believe that Tisa actually had the nerve to show her face. But then again, it was to be expected. And what's even worse is that she brought her fake tears with her. She was the reason grandma had a bad heart in the first place. I dismissed myself from her presence and stepped into the kitchen with Aunt Tee-Ona and the rest of the family.

Although Uncle Willie wasn't related by blood, he cared a great deal for our family. He called a family meeting to discuss the well being of me and Ty.

One thing that a lot of family members don't like about Uncle Willie is that he doesn't sugar coat anything. He lays it all bare. And that is exactly what he did in the meeting.

The main points that he made was that the only mother Ty and I have ever known is now gone. And when the family members start packing up their bags to go back home---mine and Ty's bags need to be packed too. The question was, who will we be going home with.

Tisa recommended that we come and stay with her. But Uncle Willie pointed out the fact that although she was our biological mother, she has never been there for us. Needless to say that Tisa didn't appreciate Uncle Willie's comments.

He asked the family to vote on what would be best for me and Ty. Out of respect for Tisa, the family voted that she make the decision regarding where Ty and I would be going. Uncle Willie didn't particularly agree with their decision but he was significantly outnumbered.

Tisa stated that Ty had to come and live with her because he was not old enough to make his own decision as to where he wanted to stay. As for me, she told me that she was sorry for not being a good mother and how much she loves me and Ty. However, she knows that I don't care much for her and being that I was seventeen years old, I was old enough to decide for myself who I wanted to stay with.

All eyes were now on me. I wanted so badly to not be separated from Ty but I just could not see myself living with Tisa.

I announced to everyone that I wanted to go to Chicago to stay with Aunt Tee-Ona and Uncle Willie and that I wanted Ty to come with me.

Tisa was fuming at this point and she insisted that I go to Chicago but Ty was not coming.

"Are you sure about this Daija?" asked Aunt Tee-Ona.

I gave it a little more thought. I had already lost Grandma Ginetta and I don't think I could deal with losing Ty too. We've had out spats every now and then, but that's my brother and I love him to death. I figured that I only have less than a year of high school left. It's gonna be hard. But for the sake of not being separated from Ty, I'll put up with Tisa for two semesters. And then I can move out and get my own place and Ty can move in with me.

"I changed my mind." I announced. "I'll go stay with Tisa."

"Oh no she won't!" Tisa blurted out, "Yall take that lil stupid heifer to Chicago with yall! That's what yall wanted anyway!" Tisa got up and went outside.

The whole family was in shock after hearing the words that just came out of Tisa's mouth. And so was I. They then decided that it was best that I go stay with Uncle Willie and Aunt Tee-Ona.

After the funeral, there were so many people that I wanted to say goodbye to. But time wouldn't allow it.

I did get the opportunity to call Mr. Davenport earlier down at the band hall and thank him for all of the inspiration and words of encouragement and for always pushing me to do and be my best.

Angela and her parents were at the funeral. I was able to say a brief farewell to them. Angela and I promised to stay in contact with each other and hopefully see each other at Howard in the fall.

Last and most importantly, I was able to spend some extremely emotional minutes with Ty. We promised to keep in touch, no matter what. I also promised him that after I got out of school, he could come and live with me. And that was a promise that I had every intent to keep.

It's amazing how a person's life can change in the blink of an eye. All of a sudden, there were many facets of my life that embraced uncertainty.

Before Grandma died, I had it all planned out. I would graduate from high school. Attend Howard University on a full academic scholarship. Graduate college and make something of myself. Come back home and spend crazy money trying to spoil Grandma Ginetta and my kid brother. Now, only God knows what the future holds for me and Ty.

I remembered the words that the ambulance driver said to me when they were taking grandma into the emergency room. "God will never put anything on you that you can't handle." It was those words that got me through my darkest hours. And I continuously allow them to resonate in my heart, mind and spirit.

Chapter
Seven

Uncle Willie and Aunt Tee-Ona lived in a nice two-story house that was located in a high-class neighborhood in the south suburbs of Chicago.

The crime rates were significantly lower in the suburbs than they were in the city. However, most parents could only dream of raising their children in a suburban environment . Point blank----if you didn't make at least fifty thousand dollars a year the likelihood of you raising a child in the suburbs was virtually non-existent.

Deaven and I had developed a close relationship. I think the fact that we were the same age had a lot to do with that. He introduced me to a lot of his friends. Mostly guys. They were out of this world fine. And they knew it. Initially, I was a little withdrawn and anti-social. Mainly because I felt out of place amongst all of these rich kids. But as the year progressed, I learned to just be myself.

Aunt Tee-Ona spent her days down in the basement doing hair and bragging to her clients about me and Deaven. And Uncle Willie was a hospital administrator at a huge Chicago hospital. When he wasn't running the hospital, he was managing his many apartment complexes. We barely saw him except for a few brief minutes on Saturdays when he would make us all get up and go out to breakfast as a family. And for a couple of hours on Sunday when we went to church as a family.

I loved my new family. But I missed my old family. I had written to Ty numerous times, to no avail. I honestly believe that Tisa was not giving him my letters. They didn't have a telephone so the only time anybody heard from Tisa was when, and if, she decided to call collect. And out of spite, when she did call, she wouldn't let me talk to Ty. She would always tell Aunt-Tee Ona that he was out with his friends or any other excuse she could think of to keep me and Ty apart. The pain of not being able to see or hear from my little brother cut like a knife. But I allowed the memories to serve as band aids to cover up the emotional wounds.

To make matters worse, my high school guidance counselor was guiding me right to a GED. She informed me that I had to attend my new school for a minimum of 3 semesters in order to graduate. So , I had two options. I could either stay an extra year by repeating the twelfth grade so that I could graduate. Or I could finish twelfth grade this year and NOT graduate. Not much to choose from if you ask me.

Aunt-Tee Ona decided that it would be best if I went ahead and completed the school year. And after school was out, I could go get my GED and go to college. It wasn't exactly what I had planned. But then again---- none of the other events that had taken place were what I had planned either.

I'm sure Aunt Tee-Ona meant well. It's just that after working so hard to make it through school for twelve years and maintaining a 4.0 GPA, I wanted my high school diploma to show for it. What child wouldn't? To me, a GED indicated that you were a high school drop out. And I was far from that.

I tried with all my might to persuade my aunt and uncle to allow me to do whatever I needed to do to get my high school diploma but it was all in vain.   Deaven was on his way to college and they wanted me on my way too. After all, that was the plan. I was to stay there and finish up my senior year and head off to college. And so it was.

Chapter
<u>Eight</u>

Howard didn't accept GED's. So I ended up going to Valley State University. It was located smack dead in the heart of Mississippi. It wasn't as big and prestigious as Howard, but it had its highlights. The student population was right around three thousand.

Uncle Willie and Aunt Tee-Ona were Valley graduates. Seeing as how they turned out alright, it can't be too bad. They knew the band director on a personal level. So, after explaining to him my predicament, he worked with me on getting a full band scholarship.

Auditioning for the scholarship was the easy part. The hard part was the behind-the-scenes string pulling that the band director had to do in order to get me accepted in the college with a GED.

Angela and I managed to stay in contact with one another. We were supposed to have been Howard roommates. So I have to admit that I was a little disappointed to not be going to Howard. Despite that, I was still excited to be attending college.

Valley State was like a whole new world for me. I was in this new place all by myself and almost a thousand miles away from my closest family.

Uncle Willie had set the ground rules before they left from dropping me off. "Keep your grades up. Your legs closed. Make sure you call collect twice a month to let us know that your doing ok. And you have to learn to budget. Since we have to pay Deavens tuition, money is going to be tight. So we will only be sending you money once a month. If you let your money run out, you'll have to do without until you get more. It's called learning responsibility."

I thought these were pretty fair rules to live by.

I spent my first day in the dormitory trying to fix up my room. The dorm rooms were very nice. There was plush green carpet on the floors. Built in cherry wood closets with matching desks on each side of the room. And two twin beds per room. The only thing thing that I didn't like about the dorm were the bright white brick walls and the fact that you had to go all the way down the hall to use the toilet or to take a shower. All of the rooms were cable ready. But there were no telephones except the payphones in the hallway.

My roommate had not arrived yet. So I was fortunate enough to have first choice on what side of the room I wanted. Being that this was a corner room, it had two windows. I decided to go for the side of the room that had the windows. Not that I was being selfish or anything. But Aunt Tee-Ona had given me a few of her houseplants to bring with me so that I could decorate my room. They needed a lot of sunlight to stay healthy. I'm sure my roommate will understand that.

Directly across from one window on the other side of the street was the cafeteria, which was located on the main strip. And through my other window I could see the student plaza that was located in front of the student union.

School didn't officially start for two more weeks. Therefore, there wasn't really a whole lot to see or do. After I finished embellishing my room, I had the rest of the day to prepare for the first day of band camp.

As I opened the blinds so that my plants could get some sunlight, I could see people starting to accumulate in front of the cafeteria. Mostly guys. They looked like football players.

I decided to sit in my room and watch BET on the color TV that Aunt Tee-Ona had bought for me. I was getting a little hungry but I wasn't about to go to the cafeteria with all of those guys. I was too embarrassed.

A few minutes passed. And when I looked out of my window again I could see that the guys were no longer in front of the cafeteria. Guess they finally got in. Suddenly, I heard some commotion in the hallway. Me being the nosy person that I am---I peeped my head out the door to see what was going on and got smacked in the head with a water balloon. Some of my dormmates were having a water fight and I got caught in the middle.

"I'm so sorry!! cried one of the girls.

The other girls were about to burst into laughter.

"I guess I did need a little cooling off," I replied humorously while attempting to shake myself dry.

"You would think that we would have air conditioning in these dorms," I stated, in an attempt to make conversation.

"Yeah. I heard it gets to be pretty hot down here in the delta. What's your name?"

"Daija."

"That's a pretty name. Where are you from?"

"Chicago, by way of Mississippi."

I was hoping that they didn't want to know too much

more about me because I didn't feel like explaining my whole life story.

"Well Daija-- my name is Rosalyn. And these are my friends Monique and Tamara. Monique and I are here for band camp. And Tamara is in cheerleader camp."

They were all from Tennessee and had graduated from the same high school.

Tamara and Monique were very pretty. They could have both passed for cheerleaders. Rosalyn, on the other hand, could have passed for a football player. Not just any football player. More like a line-backer. The girl was huge. But she had a pretty face.

After getting a little more acquainted with one another, we decided to all go to the cafeteria for dinner.

The football players were still in the cafeteria. Some of them were still eating. But most of them were just sitting around socializing to keep from going back out in the heat.

As we stood in line to get our plates some of players directed their attention our way.

Tamara nudged me in the side, "Girl they lookin at us."

I started to turn around.

"Don't look....Don't Look" she shrieked.

We continued sliding our trays down the buffet line. After we had made our way to a table to sit down, I was able to sneak a peak to see if the guys were worth all of that Drama Tamara just had in the buffet line.

"They are kinda cute." I whispered to Tamara.

"Slap ya mama cute" she winked.

Rosalyn was foaming at the mouth. I don't know if it was because she was getting ready to eat or if it was because the guys had caught her attention too.

Monique, on the other hand, was flirting with one of them and giving him the eye.

Although everybody always tell me how pretty I am, I have a hard time believing it. I've never had a boy-friend. I've never kissed a guy. And flirting was out of my league. For that reason, I didn't touch it. However, Monique appeared to be a pro at it.

Three of the guys stopped by our table after putting up their trays. The one that Monique was flirting with was one of them. He and Monique struck up a conversation.

"Yall cheerleaders?" one of them asked.

Tamara was quick to let him know that she was the only cheerleader in the group, which sparked a conversation between them.

"And we're in the band." Rosalyn intervened.

"Where yall from?" asked the last man standing.

"Memphis and Chicago." exclaimed Rosalyn.

"Who's from Chicago?"

I raised my hand.

"What part?"

"South Suburbs." I replied.

"Oh, you one of them suburban chics. Go head homegirl. I ain't mad at ya."

Turns out he was from the Chicago suburbs too.

"The names Tyrick."

"Nice to meet you Tyrick." I muttered while trying to chew my food.

I know a lady isn't supposed to talk with food in her mouth, but it was something about this guy that I didn't like. It's like our spirits clashed. I was hoping that I could gross him out enough for him to leave.

"Oh, you not gone tell me your name?" he asked.

"Daija."

"Well nice to meet you too Daija. I'll see you around."

"And my name is Rosalyn! Nice to meet you too----with your fine self." she mumbled under her breathe.

"Yall c'mon man. We gone be late for practice." Tyrick yelled as he headed for the cafeteria door.

Monique and Tamara's newfound friends followed behind him.

After we finished eating, Rosalyn, Monique, and Tamara went to hang out at the student union for a while. As for me, I decided to go back to my room so I could rest up for band camp tomorrow. I knew that if it was anything like high school band camp, I was going to need all the rest I could get--and then some.

Besides--Rosalyn and company were on a manhunt and I didn't want any parts of it.

Chapter
Nine

I quickly became friends with nearly everyone in the band. It kinda reminded me of how it was in high school. Makes one wonder if all bands are this way. One big happy family.

We practiced every day during band camp from five thirty in the morning till almost midnight. I wasn't in the best of shape before coming to camp. But all of this practicing and marching up and down the football field during practice had forced me into shape. And on top of that, I had turned three shades darker from being outside in that Mississippi delta sun all day.

Most nights after getting out of practice everybody would just go back to the dorms, shower, and go to sleep. But weekends were a different story. Everybody would sit and hang out on the yard to relax and socialize.

The ones who had boyfriends or girlfriends would go to the local hotel. Those who couldn't afford to go to the hotel would sneak into one another's dorm rooms late at night. Or go to this old abandoned airport on a dark backroad. Tamara, Rosalyn and Monique were among them.

I just couldn't get down with all of that. I got saved at an early age. I knew that I wasn't perfect, but I tried to do most of the things the bible said do. I was still a virgin. A proud one. And I planned to stay that way until I got married.

Every now and then I would see Tyrick hanging out on campus. He would always be hanging around with his football clique. If I saw him before he saw me, I would try my best to go the opposite direction. He was too flirty for me. And he would always try to embarrass people if they didn't respond favorably to his sexist comments.

And there was still something else about him that just didn't seem right. But I couldn't put my finger on it.

By the time school officially started, I had made quite a few acquaintances. Some good and some bad. But I had to put all of that aside and start thinking about the real reason that I was there. To get an education.

I still hadn't decided on what I was gonna major in. I didn't even know what all of the fields of study were for Valley. So I decided to seek the advice of Uncle Willie. The big money man. I put my one phone call per month to use.

He suggested that I major in accounting or a business related field because that's were the money was. Computer Science was another option.

Aunt Tee-Ona was more concerned with me majoring in something that I was interested in.

Her advice---"Money isn't everything. Your uncle's advice is good. But you need to major in something that you like. Not something he likes. Before you decide on your major, think about whether or not it's going to be something that you won't mind doing everyday for twenty five or thirty years."

I have to admit that Aunt Tee-Ona's advice appealed to me a lot more than Uncle Willie's.

After I got off the phone, I started trying to think of something that I wouldn't mind doing for the rest of my life. Then all of a sudden, it came to me. Music! That was it. It was something I loved. And it was like a hobby for me. I would absolutely love to become a band director. So I guess that major would be called Music Education.

Chapter Ten

My popularity with the guys slowly skyrocketed. Most of them referred to me as "fresh meat." The fact that I was still a virgin had a lot to do with that.

I had been out on a few dates. Initially they pretended to respect my intentions to remain pristine until I got married. It was a way for them to get their foot in the door. But most of them ending up dumping me because they wanted sex and I didn't.

I knew there were a few good men still out there. But most of them were already spoken for. Clayton was one of them.

He and I marched next to each other in the band. He was the best drummer we had. And in no time, we had become best friends.

He was very charismatic. And, if I may add--quite handsome. Everybody can't sport a baldhead. But Clayton was working it. A big waxed chocolate milkdud. And his eyes were framed with long dark curly eyelashes. They were so perfect, God must have placed them on his face one by one. He wasn't really a dressy kind of guy. He would mostly sport a tee shirt and a nice pair of Levi's that accentuated his physique.

Clayton seemed to know everything that women wanted. Charm appeared to come second nature to him. He was what Grandma Ginetta would have referred to as a ladies man. Always flirting. Especially with the girls in the band. But he swore up and down that he was being faithful to his girlfriend back home. Sometimes I wondered if he really did have a girlfriend.

His parents had money. And I honestly believe that he became my friend out of sympathy.

Being that I had to budget the fifty dollars a month that I received from Uncle Willie, I didn't really have room for splurging. I never went out with my peers if the activities they were engaging in required money. And whenever we went on band trips, I would always have to wait for the free meals before I could eat.

Apparently Clayton noticed these things and he started buying me stuff. Every now and then, he would even slip a twenty-dollar bill in my hand. I didn't like taking things from him. I've always heard the older women say that as soon as you start taking handouts from a man--that's when they start to get territorial. But he insisted that "That's what friends are for."

It was shocking for me to discover that so many people on campus were jealous of mine and Clayton's friendship.

The ladies acted as if I was a thorn in their sides that blew any chances of them staking their claim on him. And trust me. They wanted him baaaad. A good looking brother with wealthy parents. He was a gold-iggers heaven.

The fellows, on the other hand, were jealous for a completely different reason altogether. They would stare at us with that "I can't believe she lettin him hit that but won't even give me the time of day" look.

It was quite obvious that they didn't understand the true nature of mine and Clayton's relationship. And that really and truly bothered me. I had a reputation to maintain. And I didn't want people to think we were sleeping together. I didn't mind the part about them thinking Clayton and I were a couple. It was actually kind of flattering. Especially when strangers walked up to us exclaiming, "Aww--You guys look so cute together."

I just didn't want the fellows on campus to think I was loose. Do you know how fast a rumor like that can spread? It didn't bother Clayton though. He was soaking it all in. Seemingly enjoying every minute of it.

"People are gonna believe what they wanna believe. So why try to deter their narrow little minds. As long as you and I know the real deal, forget about everybody else." That would always be his take on the situation.

Every now and then I would imagine that Clayton and I were really a couple. We got along well. I could talk to him about anything. He was caring. Faithful. Intelligent. Attractive. Oh--and did I say faithful?

Yeah--that's the part that always jolts me back into reality. He already has a girlfriend and he' s faithful. She's a lucky woman. Good men like him are hard to find. He was two steps away from perfect. And I say that because first of all, nobody's perfect. And second of all, there was one flaw in Clayton's character that I didn't particularly care for. He had a quick temper. Not with me. Because when he was around me, he poured on the charm. But I had witnessed him going off on other people quite a few times.

Sometimes he clowned so bad that he made ME want to cry. His cussin outs weren't gender biased. It didn't matter if you were male of female. And he didn't mind putting you in check in a public place. Wherever you happen to be when you step on his toes, that's exactly where he will get you off of them.

Whenever I suggested that maybe he was a little too hard on people, his response would always be, "I'm a man. And a man ain't gonna sit back and let nobody disrespect him. That's just who I am."

I couldn't really argue with him there. Who was I to say how a man was supposed to act? My father was never around. I was never exposed to the 'how a man is suppose to act' rulebook. So I just let Clayton be Clayton.

Chapter Eleven

After finally getting tired of getting my hopes up and my heart broken, I decided to throw in the towel. Looking for Mr. Right on this campus was almost a mission impossible. It seemed that most of the guys had a one way brain whose streets led straight down the path to sex.

But wouldn't you know that as soon as I gave up my quest to find Mr. Right--this guy that was too good to be true walked right into my life. His name was Judge. Judge Carter.

Normally I wouldn't date anyone of a high yellow complexion. Mainly because they were notorious for being the pretty boys on campus who ended up dogging out the girls that they were with. And Initially I did, in fact, have my reservations about him. He seemed so perfect. Life lessons had already taught me that if something seems too good to be true--it probably is. But for some strange reason, I chose to ignore my intuition and I let my guard down.

Judge came off as being a real low-key kind of guy. He gave me a long story about how he was celibate because he was focusing on his relationship with God. Those words were music to my ears. He had a relationship with God and he wasn't out for sex. Exactly the kind of guy I was interested in. He had a gift of gab that just reached out and grabbed me. I've always been a sucker for a charmer.

I thought he was "the one." But I later discovered that he was somehow affiliated with Tyrick. I would spot them socializing on occasion.

A little bad blood had developed between me and Tyrick. He housed a lot of animosity towards me because I refused to succumb to his sexual advances.

As much as Tyrick urked my soul, I couldn't understand for the life of me how I could KNOWINGLY be falling for one of his acquaintances. Birds of a feather flock together. Or at least that's what I heard.

I tried to compare Judge and Tyricks relationship to mine and Rosalyn's.

I mean look at her and look at me. The girls a sexaholic. I'm a virgin. She and I just had a long discussion the other day after she informed me that she had found her a new bed buddy. She didn't seem to mind having relationships that were specifically of a sexual nature.

Everytime I tried to confront her about her promiscuity, her rebuttal would always be "Girl if you can't beat em--bed em." We're like day and night we're so different. Maybe Judge and Tyrick are the same way.

After a few months of dating, Judge had me so far gone in the head that my acceptance of his affiliation with Tyrick wasn't the only thing that surpassed my understanding. My nose was so wide open that I actually went into a yearbook. Cut out the boy's picture. Wrapped it in aluminum foil.

Punched a hole in it. And wore it around my neck as a pendant. If that's not gone, I don't know what is.

I was curious to know why he wasn't well known on campus. Normally a guy like him would have the ladies fighting all over him. But most of the girls who saw his picture around my neck wanted to know who he was.

One night Rosalyn decided she wanted to make a creep down to the male's dormitory to see her partner. She asked me to go with her because she didn't want to walk down there by herself.

"Have you lost your mind? I'm not going to the boys' dormitory! And you better not go either... What if someone sees you?"

She assured me that she wouldn't get caught.

"Why don't you just ask Monique or Tamara to go with you?"

"They're busy trying to take care of their own business. Look---I go down there all the time. Nobody's gonna see us Daija. I promise. Besides Judge lives in the same suite as my man and you know you want to see him, while you trying to act all holier than thou. Stop trippin."

Peer pressure is a terrible thing. It also happened to be one of my weaknesses. And I have to admit that I wouldn't mind seeing Judge.

"Alright, I'll walk down there with you. But I'm not going in. When you get in, you can just tell Judge that he has a visitor outside."

"It's a deal," she agreed.

We went down to the boys' dorm covered in black from head to toe. It was supposed to prevent us from being seen.

Once we got there, we spotted a security car pulling out of the parking lot in front of the boys' dorm.

"Quick, we're gonna have to go up the side stairwell before security comes back through here and sees us."

"No. You go up the side stairwell. I told you I wasn't going in."

Rosalyn then enlightened me that if security caught a female standing outside the males' dorm at this time of night, they would write them a quick ticket out of here.

Of course I am fuming right about now. But I didn't have much of a choice. It was either stand outside and get caught by security. Or go up the stairwell and risk damaging my reputation.

"Are you sure that I won't get into trouble?" I asked seeking some sort of reassurance.

"Only if we get caught, " she said as she started snickering.

"Ok---forgive me for not seeing the humor in all of this."

"Dang Daija! Stop being so sedity. Just relax. and follow me."

I followed her up the side stairwells all the way up to the fifth floor. When we got to the fifth floor, we stopped to take a breather. We could see all the way down the hall through the end door that was propped open. And although it was extremely noisy, there wasn't a soul in sight.

"I'm gonna go knock on the suite door and I'll beckon for you once the door is open. You can't stand out here on the stairwell because if you do someone will see you?"

"Alright."

Seemed like it took forever for Rosalyn to get someone to open the door. After she beckoned for me, I made a run for it.

The fear of getting caught had my heart racing a hundred miles per hour as I made my way to the suite door. But once I entered the suite I was stopped dead in my tracks as my heart came to a screeching halt.

It was Tyrick.

And Rosalyn was all up on him. Not that I cared--but I can't believe that she would stoop that low. And even worse, I can't believe she didn't tell me. I thought our friendship was better than that.

"Well, well well...if it isn't little miss virginity! What are you doing in the boys dormitory?"

"It's none of your business. And Rosalyn we need to talk."

Tyrick continued, "Au Contraire. Seeing as how you're dating my cousin, I think it is my business."

I cocked my head to the side in total confusion.

"What are you talking about?"

"Oh Judge didn't tell you?" he asked with a smirk on his face as he proceeded to yell out Judge's name to get him to open the door.

Judge opened up the door before I could turn around and leave. "Yo man—look what the wind blew in."

Judge appeared somewhat surprised to see me as Tyrick and Rosalyn made their exit.

I couldn't believe she just left me standing there like that. When we get back to the dorm, I am going to really give her a piece of my mind. With the stunts that she has pulled tonight, I think we need to reevaluate our friendship.

"What are you doing here?" Judge inquired.

I gave him the rundown on how Rosalyn had begged me to walk down here with her. "Well I'm glad you came, I was just thinking about you. Come on in."

"I shouldn't. It just doesn't feel right."

As I turned around to leave, he grabbed my arm in an attempt to stop me, "C'mon, you're here now, so you may as well stay a while. Besides--I was just looking out my window and security is patrolling the area right now. It wouldn't be wise to go back down those stairs until they have left the vicinity. "

As much as I wanted to leave, I definitely didn't want to be caught by security. "Fine, I'll come in. But only until security is gone."

I followed as he led me by the hand into his room that wreaked with the scent of dirty, sweaty socks and funky underwear. I felt the pressure rising in my throat. And it took everything within me to keep down the vomit. How could a person live under such conditions?

I couldn't believe that as perfect as Judge presented himself to be, he lived in a room that smelled worse than pig chitterlings.

He hit the lights and let up the window up so that the air could circulate. It's almost as if he knew that his room smelled foul but just didn't care.

I didn't particularly want to be in the dark. But it was either let the window stay up with the lights turned off so fresh air could come in. Or turn the lights back on and let the window back down and smell all the fumes in this funk factory. A catch twenty-two. I needed air.

I eased over to the window to escape the stinge before I passed out from holding my breathe. The view was great. I could see the entire campus. And sure enough, security was still patrolling the boys' dorm.

"So why didn't you tell me that you and Tyrick were cousins?" I tried to remain calm.

"Didn't think it mattered." he answered rather non-chalantly.

"You mean to tell me that as many times that I have told you about how uneasy I get when he's around--you didn't think it mattered? Is this suppose to be a game or something?"

"Daija, I don't want to argue over something so petty. Dang, it's not that big of a deal!"

That's when all hell broke loose. I know this Negro did not just yell at me. This character that I thought was so perfect was finally starting to show his true colors.

After arguing back and forth for a few minutes, I was ready to give him the boot. Mainly because he yelled at me. Also because I felt there was a little more to why he didn't inform me that he and Tyrick were cousins.

"You know what? I thought you were different from the other guys around here. But I was wrong. You're no better than they are. I'm leaving."

As I headed for the door, he grabbed me from behind and threw me down on the bed.

"You know you want me. You wouldn't be here if you didn't."

I tried to get up but he pushed me back down and climbed on top of me. He secured my hands above my head as he started kissing me. I had never kissed a guy before, but I knew that it wasn't supposed to be like this.

"Stop it Judge!! Get off of me. You're scaring me!"

"What are you gonna do? Run and tell security that I drug you all the way up to the fifth floor and made you come in my room? Lay back and enjoy it. You know you want it."

He started fondling parts of my body that were sacred to me. Parts that I didn't want him seeing or touching. And no matter how hard I tried to fight him off, he was too overbearing. I kept screaming for help in hopes that Rosalyn or someone would come to my rescue.

As he made his way down and started unzipping my pants, I tried even harder to fight back. But I was still unsuccessful. He rammed himself inside of me. The last thing I remembered was looking at the red digital numbers on the clock that read 10:31. I blacked out. When I came to, I glanced at the clock to see how much time had passed. 10:34.

Judge had unmounted me and was standing over me as I still lay there paralyzed on the bed in a state of shock.

"Security's gone. You can leave now." he mumbled as if nothing had ever happened.

I was speechless. I felt humiliated and violated.

After putting my clothes back on, I left. I didn't care about Rosalyn or anybody else. I just wanted to be alone. I slowly made my way down the stairwells in such a state of shock that I wasn't even paying attention to who saw me. Nor did I care.

The walk back from the boys' dorm to my room was a walk of death. With each step that I took, I lost a piece of myself as I kept replaying what had just happened over and over in my mind.

How could I let this happen?

Words can't begin to express how low I feel right now. The only thing that I had that was of value to me I just lost. And I can never get it back.

When I got back to my dorm I was so out of it that I headed straight for the shower. Shoes and all.

I remember standing in the shower under the hot running water, clothes soaking wet. Crying and wishing that the water could just wash away the pain .

I don't know how long I stayed in there, but when I came out a girl that was in the hall saw me. She looked as if she wanted to say something to me but instead she just stared.

Still in a trance, I glared at her and kept walking towards my room. When I got there, I didn't bother getting out of my clothes. I just fell across my bed and cried until there were no more tears left.

I started having mental conversations with myself. Thoughts of Grandma Ginetta's passing kept coming back to the forefront of my mind. I wished she were still here. I wish I could talk to her. I wish I could hug her. But I can't. And it's my fault. If I had given her that pill she would be here right now…

I creeped over to the closet and pulled down my brown paper bag with Grandma Ginetta's dress in it from that night. I closed my eyes as I sat back down on the bed and smelled it. It still had her scent on it.

Why did she have to leave me here? I need her so much.

I suddenly remembered the bottle of sleeping pills that Aunt Tee-Ona had bought for me before I came down here. I can end it right now. Right here.

I got back up and got the bottle of pills. Before I knew it, I had downed the whole bottle. I remember thinking that it would soon be over as I lie back down on the bed hoping that I would fall asleep and never wake up.

For some reason, I didn't die. I slept for a day and a half-- but I didn't die. I awoke to Rosalyn bamming on my door like a madwoman trying to see if I was alright.

I didn't open my door. I didn't want to see anybody and I didn't want to talk to anyone. Especially her. I didn't eat or go to class for over a week. The only time I came out of my room was to use the bathroom. I didn't shower. Didn't comb my hair or brush my teeth. I looked like hell. But I didn't care because I also felt like hell. And the pain was still there.

After running out of the ramen noodles I had stored in my room, I finally came out to go to the cafeteria. But I still didn't talk to anyone.

Everyone I passed stared at me wondering why I looked like I had been in combat with someone. And although I knew that people were around me, it's like they weren't there. I was in my own little world.

I found me a table that was secluded way back in a corner away from the crowd. As I sat there all alone, head bowed, eating stale spaghetti and sipping on my kool-aid, this stranger walked up to my table. He stood there a couple of seconds before saying anything.

I was so depressed and out of it, that I couldn't bring myself to lift up my head and see his face. So he knelt down beside my chair and put his hand on my shoulder.

"You don't know me personally," he stated. "But I know you. And I know that you normally walk around this campus with your head high and a big ole smile on your face. You look like you got a lot of pressures weighing you down right now. But I just wanted to tell you that God won't put anything on you that you can't handle."

He now had my attention. Because that was the same thing the ambulance driver had said to me the night Grandma Ginetta died.

He then took his hand off of my shoulder and gently touched my chin to lift my head up. "Now can I get a smile?"

As much as I wanted to resist smiling, I found myself give a little smile back at him.

He then looked into my eyes. And it seemed as if he could see straight through to the depths of my soul and knew all of the heartache and pain that was inside of me.

I felt a tear starting to fall down my cheek.   "Thank you." I whispered.

And with that, he got up and left. I had never seen this guy a day in my life. And I never saw him again. But, I honestly believe that God had sent me an angel that day.

Chapter
Twelve

I eventually told Uncle Willie and Aunt Tee-Ona about what Judge did to me. If I didn't know better I would have thought that they were placing all of the blame on me.

They were more concerned over the thought of me being in the boys' dormitory than they were about bringing him to justice. They wanted me to keep quiet about it. According to them no one would ever believe that I was really raped --seeing as how I did take it upon myself to go to his room. And God forbid if word got around that their niece was running around in the mens dormitory. It would damage their unblemished reputations. But as much as it hurt--I listened to them.

To preserve their reputations, I tried to lay all of my feelings aside and follow their advice. But it was humanly impossible. I couldn't turn my feelings off with the flick of a lightswitch. So I ended up burying those feelings deep down in my heart. And although it hurt, I never told anyone else about it. I let it go. I pretended it never happened and went on with my life.

I reevaluated a lot of friendships. And cut off a lot of people who didn't mean me any good. Rosalyn was one of them. I never told her why. I just let our relationship slowly drift apart until it no longer existed.

Clayton was the only person that I didn't completely cut off. I felt like I could trust him. But I did find myself trying to limit the amount of time we spent together. It was dangerous for my heart. The more time we spent together--the more I wished and longed for someone like him in my life. But I knew I couldn't have him because his heart was with someone else.

Of course I still had Angela to chat with every now and then. She had met her prince charming up at Howard U. He was a medical student. They were engaged and living together in an on campus apartment. We would always joke about how her parents would hit the ceiling if they ever found out.

"What they don't know won't hurt em," was Angela's take on it.

They had just bought her a new car. And she was making plans to come down and visit me during homecoming week. I was really looking forward to it. We would be able to kick it again like old times. She was also trying to persuade her fiancé to come along for the ride. And although I really wanted to meet this guy that had come along and swept my best friend off of her feet, I was kinda hoping he wouldn't come.

I know that sounds selfish. But I haven't seen Angela since Grandma Ginetta's funeral. And I didn't want to be competing with her fiancé for her attention. We had so much to catch up on.

Chapter
Thirteen

Homecoming week was a blur--as it always is. But I had a great time. In fact, it was the best time I've had the whole three years I've been here.

Angela didn't bring her fiancé with her. He had other engagements that he had committed to. So we just kicked it like old times. And it felt good to be able to sit down and reminisce with my best friend. There was so much that both of us had to catch up on.

We talked about how much fun she was having at Howard and how nightlife was in the big city for a 21-year-old. She cheerfully went on and on giving me all of the extravagant details.

My mind begin to wander off. Her talking slowly faded into the background of my mind as I started daydreaming about what possibly could have been-- had I actually gone to Howard with Angela. I got to thinking about how hard I was trying to stick to my Christian ethics that Grandma Ginetta had instilled in me. Wondering was it worth it. Seems like I've had a lifetime of pain by trying to do the right thing. But all of my friends are having the time of their life with no concerns about the consequences. Even Angela was living with a man whom she wasn't married to. And where Angela and I came from, that was a big no no. Old folks called it "shacking".

Angela knows that. But look at her. She's so happy.

"Daija--are you listening to me?"

"Huh?"

" I said--who's the lucky guy?"

"Lucky guy?"

"Girl don't front like you don't have your eye on one of these tantalizing chocolate morsels walking around here."

"Whatever!" I exclaimed while trying not to blush. And I don't know why in the world thoughts of Clayton started dancing around in my head. Well--actually I do. But that's beside the point. He's marked territory.

"There is no lucky guy." I was still trying to keep a straight face. But I knew it wasn't working.

"You know I can tell when you're lying. Don't you?" Angela pointed out.

I couldn't hold out any longer. So I finally gave in and gave her the 411 on Clayton. Including the fact that he had a girlfriend.

"Did he put a ring on her finger?"

"No. Not that I know of." I replied.

"Well. Obviously he's still not sure if she's the one. Because if he was sure, she would have a ring. But seeing as how she doesn't--he's fair game. I should know. That's how I landed Derrick. And now I have his ring on my finger. And she's---well---history. So you can sit back and sing the 'he got a girlfriend' song if you want to. See where it gets you."

"What if he's not interested?"

"If he's not interested, you still live to see another day. At least you'll know and won't be sitting around thinking about what could have been."

I knew Angela was right, but I couldn't help but ponder on the fact that the entire three years that Clayton and I have been friends, he has never acted as if he was even remotely interested in having a relationship with me. Although he flirted with me a lot, he couldn't be taken seriously because he flirts with everybody.

I had arranged for Clayton to meet Angela. Of course, I had to make Angela promise not to be throwing out her subliminal hints to Clayton about me liking him. He's a smart one and he would catch on quick.

"Umph—he is wearing those those levi's. If you don't go after that, I'll ditch Derrick and go after him myself."

"You're crazy girl!"

I'll never understand why people get so wrapped up in the way a person looks. I was falling for Clayton because he treated me better than any man I ever knew. He was always there to lend a helping hand. His looks were just icing on the cake. A person can be butt-ugly as long as they treat me right.

And I have to be honest and say that after the whole Judge ordeal, it's scary to think of myself being involved with any guy. I think part of me was in denial that the rape ever happened.

The urge to tell Angela what Judge did to me was eating away at my soul like acid. But I had to restrain that desire. I knew if I told her, she would have told her mother--no matter how much I made her swear to secrecy. And knowing Angela's mother as I do, she wouldn't hesitate to put her law degree to use.

The last thing Aunt Tee-Ona and Uncle Willie would want to hear about is me being caught up in some legal battle all because I took my behind down to the boys' dorm. I promised them that I wouldn't tell anyone about what happened.

It's amazing how a person will put their own inner peace on the back burner so that they can try and keep the peace with others. I would never do anything to upset the little family that I did have left.

After the homecoming game, Angela and I had a few moments to exchange hugs and say a little prayer for her safe return back to Washington.

"You need to pursue that man. Don't make me have to come back down here and hook y'all up." She winked at me and climbed into her little red Honda Accord.

I just shook my head as I stood there with my hands in my pockets watching her car disappear into the distance. It had been a long weekend, so I went back to retire at the dorm.

Chapter
Fourteen

"You broke up with her?"

I tried to hide the exhilaration in my voice. I had been waiting almost four years for this moment. So hiding my excitement and pretending to be empathetic of Clayton's situation was an extremely difficult task to overcome.

While he was giving me the 'why we didn't work out spill', my attention was focused elsewhere. I was creating a mental blueprint of how I was going to make him mine in so little time. Time was literally slipping through my fingers as graduation day slowly approached.

I had less than eight months left to make him mine. Difficult--but not impossible.

As I was sitting there having mental conversations with myself, his voice resurfaced in the foreground.

"So will you go with me?"

Was he asking me out on a date? "Go with you where Clayton?"

"To the pink ice ball."

Although I'm not a dating professional, I know that a lady should never date a guy who's on the rebound. But for every rule, there is an exception. And this is an exception because that rule only applies if the rebounder is in search of prey. Surely Clayton didn't see me as prey. I honestly don't think he had a clue that I was even remotely interested in him. Besides, we've been best friends for four years. And if he couldn't ask me to go to the ball with him as a replacement for his ex-girlfriend, who could he ask?

He was Mr. Pink Ice and this was a really big event for him. And what kind of friend would I be if I weren't there for him in his time of need.

"I'd be thrilled to go with you Clayton but I don't have anything to wear."

"Don't worry about what you're gonna wear. I got that covered. All I want to know is will you go with me?"

My heart was turning flips like crazy. "Of course, I'll go with you Clayton--that's what friends are for right?"

He and I went shopping as a team for the perfect evening dress. His treat. It had to be pink or cream.

The ball was only two weeks away. So most of the good dresses had already been taken. We went to every single store in the area. I couldn't find anything to fit my 5' 6", 150-lb. frame.

Naturally I was starting to feel a little anxious. I wasn't worried about whether or not I would be able to find something decent to wear. Decent was easily obtainable. I wanted something breathtaking. Something that would literally take Clayton's breathe away.

There was one last store we hadn't hit yet. So there was still hope.

When I walked in the store, the perfect dress was right there in front of my eyes. I walked on past it because I didn't want Clayton to see it. As he browsed through the dresses that were in the back of the store, I eased my way back up to the front of the store. Size 12. Perfect!

And only $120.00. I hid the dress on a clearance rack so Clayton wouldn't stumble across it. I then discreetly beckoned for the sales lady to come to the front to assist me. Clayton never noticed.

"I'm sorry miss. But I want this dress. I have the money to buy it, but I don't want that guy back there to see it because I want it to be a surprise. Can you help me?"

"We have layaway and we have mail order," she responded.

"Well-I know layaway is out of the question because I wouldn't have a ride back over here to pick it up."

"You live that far away?"

"Actually--I don't. I go to school at Valley U. But I don't have any friends with cars except that guy back there. I can't ask him because it would ruin the surprise."

"Tell you what," she started, "Since I have to drive right past Valley to get home, if you give me your dorm number, I'll personally drop it off for you."

If that's not excellent customer service, I don't know what is.

I felt like hugging her but I didn't want Clayton to get suspicious about my excitement. I dug into my pocket to get the $150.00 that Clayton had given me and pretended to shake the sales lady hand as I discreetly transferred the money from mines to hers.

"I need some shoes too." I whispered.

"Well today must be your lucky day because we just got in the perfect pair of shoes to go with this dress. We haven't even put them on the shelves yet, so you won't have to worry about someone else wearing the same shoes."

She snuck to the back to get them.

"You find anything yet?!" I yelled to Clayton.

"No--not really. Have you? he replied, with disappointment in his voice.

"Nope. Still looking. I might have to get one of my friends to bring me back later on this weekend. The lady said they'll be getting a new shipment in on Friday."

So what. I lied. A little white lie never killed anybody. Besides--it's for a good cause.

By this time, the sales lady was making her way back up to the front of the store to show me the shoes. They were beautiful. The perfect match. I peeped at the price tag. And what do you know--they were $29.99.

"I want them."

"I figured you would," she smiled.

The total bill was $149.99. Hot dog! I had a whole penny to spare. Am I a shopper or what? She went back and prepared me a receipt. I--in turn, gave her my name, dorm number and the number for the payphone in the hall just in case.

"I'm sorry I didn't catch your name," I stated with curiosity.

"Angel." she responded

"Well that explains everything. You truly ARE an Angel. And I can't begin to tell you how much I appreciate what you're doing to help me."

I continued browsing around the store nonchalantly until Clayton decided he was ready to go. Phase 1 of my mission had been accomplished.

Chapter
Fifteen

The night has finally come. I'm wearing my beautiful pink evening gown with the shoulders out and I have a sheer pink scarf draping over my bare caramel hued skin. My hair is upswept with a wisp of hair falling in my face. Got on my clear see-through slippers. Looking like a Black Cinderella, if I must say so myself.

I was just finishing up last minute touches when, suddenly, there was a knock on my door. When I opened it, one of the girls in the dorm informed me that I had a visitor in the lobby.

Oh my goodness, Clayton was 15 minutes early. I stopped what I was doing and took a deep breathe in an attempt to pull myself together before leaving my room.

"It's gonna be ok---It's gonna be ok," I kept repeating to myself. Finally I decided to head towards the lobby.

As I entered the lobby, my mouth dropped.

Clayton had his back turned. Since he couldn't see me looking at him, I simply stood there staring in astonishment of how gorgeous he was. "Dang girl--Get it together," I kept saying to myself.

Shaking it off, I slowly proceeded down the steps to the lobby.

"You're early." I stated as I snuck up behind him.

When he turned around, my breath was, literally, taken away. For a moment, I thought this was all a dream. He was standing in my dorm lobby in a White Tuxedo, with 2 dozen pink roses in his arms looking just like an angel. His smile was as warm as sunshine. And it made my heart melt. He smelled sweeter than honey. As he presented me with me with the roses, our eyes met. And it seemed as if his eyes were like fire, burning a hole in my soul.

"You look beautiful Daija," he whispered ever so gently.

I could tell that he was just as pleasantly surprised as I was. "Ditto," I replied, still almost speechless.

He then extended his arm and I boldly put my arm in his as we proceeded to the ball. Hence the beginning of our enchanted evening. Not a bad start. Not bad at all.

We made our way to the top of the stairwell and paused at the entrance of the union ballroom. The glass doors were propped open. Keith Sweat's "right and wrong way" was blasting in the background.

I could see couples dancing. Others sitting. Pink and white balloons lie on the floor surrounding the plush red carpet that ran from the entrance all the way up to the front--where two big red velvet chairs with gold trimming sat patiently awaiting the arrival of two very important guests.

Nervousness kicked in and I started to feel a little tingle. The atmosphere was so surrealistic that I had to pinch myself to see if it was dreaming.

Ouch! That hurt. I glanced over at Clayton. He looked as cool as a cucumber. Apparently he sensed my nervousness.

"You ok?" he asked as he stared into my eyes with deep concern.

"Yeah--just a little nervous."

"Don't be." He paused and caressed my cheek, "You look beautiful."

Our eyes met for what felt like an eternity. I felt my knees get weak. "I have to run to the ladies room. I'll just be a moment."

I then excused myself from Clayton's presence by making a quick u-turn to the ladies restroom.

The student union had doorless stalls. I took the last one on the end so that I could have some privacy while I made a desperate attempt to regain my composure. I can't believe that a simple touch on the cheek affected me like that.

Breathe in. Pause. Breathe out. Breathe in. Pause. Breathe out. I repeated this cycle about ten times. The affect was the same as ammonia being put to the nose of a fainted person. I slowly started coming back to my senses.

I glanced down at my rhinestone-embellished watch. Ten minutes!! I've been in here for ten minutes?! Clayton is gonna think I was in here dropping logs. How embarrassing.

I flushed the toilet and headed back out--stopping to take a quick glance in the mirror. "You lookin like the bommmmb gurrrrrrrrrl!" I exclaimed as I blew my reflection a kiss and headed on out the door.

Clayton was still patiently standing exactly where I left him.

"Sorry I took so long. Had to powder my nose." I smiled in hopes that he believed me.

"That's alright. I know how y'all women are."

He then hooked his arm in mine and looked at me with one eyebrow raised, "You ready?"

I nodded my head in confirmation.

"Ok. Let's do this." he replied as he started navigating us toward the red carpet.

All eyes were on us as we made our grand entrance. As we gracefully approached the thrones that had been prepared for us one of the girls grabbed the microphone.

"Alright you guys! Let's give a warm welcome to Mr. Pink Ice-- Clayton Powell!"

He led me to my seat. Then went and accepted the microphone from the girl.

"Thanks everybody for that warm welcome. Most importantly, thank you all for choosing me to be this year's Mr. Pink Ice. It's truly an honor. I know some of you may be wondering who this beautiful young lady is who was kind enough to grace us--especially me-- with her presence. I'd like to introduce to you my best friend. The beautiful Ms. Daija Rogers!!! Y'all give it up for Daija!"

I could feel myself turning ten shades of red. The guys gave whistles and the females gave polite handclaps. Others just stood there and stared with eyes of envy and hateration. Justifiably so. I was a thorn in their sides that prevented them from getting close to Mr. Pink Ice. Tonight he was all mine.

After the applause and whistles stopped, the music started booming again. Clayton took his seat beside me.

He leaned over and whispered in my ear, "Hope I didn't embarrass you too bad."

"Not TOO bad." I winked.

After sitting there for a few minutes watching others dance and have a good time, Clayton took me by the hand and led me onto the dance floor. It was kind of crowded because Electric Slide was playing. And you know everybody and their momma be on the floor trying to do the electric slide.

After the Electric Slide stopped playing, the DJ put on Lenny Williams. That was my cue to head back to my seat.

"Girl you know I I I I Love youuuu--No matter what you do." The crowd was singing along.

Clayton grabbed my hand and halted me from going back to my throne. " I know you're not gonna leave me hanging on my favorite song."

He put a fake pout on his face as he pulled me in close to him and started dancing. His hands were gently caressing my waist. I wrapped my arms around his neck and placed my head on his chest. I was listening to the words of the song as we swayed from left to right.

"Cause I lovvvveee You.....I neeeeedd you. " The music continued. I felt so safe and secure with Clayton's arms holding me. My head resting on his warm chest that was pulsating the thump of his heartbeat. If I could freeze one moment in time this would be it. It was a feeling I wanted to last forever.

"May I have this dance?" this butt ugly female interjected.

She was messing up a cherished moment. This is the same girl that kept bumping into me when we were doing the electric slide. It seemed intentional but I let it go because the dance floor was so crowded and it could have been purely coincidental. But this--there was no excuse for.

Although Clayton and I were not a couple, I would like to know what in the world made her think Clayton would want to ditch me to dance with her.

Clayton's mouth flew open like he had seen a ghost.

"Charlotte--what the hell are you doing here?" he asked with the highest level of pisstivity in his voice.

Instinct told me that they knew each other on a 'more than just friends level'.

So much for that cherished moment.

"Clayton, I'm gonna go grab some punch. Want some?"

She glanced at me like she wanted to jump over and claw my eyeballs out.

"No thanks Daija--I'm cool. Don't take too long." I then looked back at her. Turned. And politely walked away. Any other time I would have clowned. But not tonight. I was looking too good to get into a scuffle with Harlot--or whatever the huzzies name was.

I stood over near the punch bowl trying to discreetly observe Clayton's body language and facial expressions. From the looks of things, the conversation was getting pretty heated. I couldn't help but wonder who this mystery girl was that was getting Clayton so worked up.

Unable to suppress my curiosity any longer, I started making my way back to the dance floor. They were so engrossed in their bickering that neither of them saw me coming. I eased over and wrapped my arm around one of his that was hanging limp at his side. Then brought up my other hand to secure the locked embrace.

Both of them directed their eyes towards me. My eyes met his with deep concern. "Everything ok Clayton?"

"Yeah--she was just leaving." he stated, as he turned his back to her and started escorting us back to our thrones.

"Clayton, don't you dare turn your back on me!!" she yelled, with tears in her eyes, as she ran up behind us and grabbed his arm.

Her outburst kindled the DJ's curiosity so much that he took the needle off the record. Everybody got quiet. And if we weren't the center of attention before, we certainly were now.

"Charlotte, don't do this. It's over." He was biting his bottom lip in an attempt to quench his anger.

"The hell it is over. If you think you can just knock me up and drop me like a hot potato, you got another think coming!"

I could hear whispers flooding the room.

"Charlotte. Let's take this outside." Clayton removed his arm from mine as he grabbed hers and headed towards the door.

She jerked away.

I thought Clayton was gonna bite his lip off. "Get your hands off of me! I know why you don't want to talk in here. It's because you don't want your peers to know what kind of low life scum you are. Mr. Pink Ice. Please nigga you ain't nothing but a punk. You cowar__

Before she could finish her sentence, she was on the floor.

I couldn't believe my eyes. Clayton had just punched her like he was Muhammad Ali fighting George Foreman.

Everyone crowded around her as Clayton stormed out of the ballroom like a madman.

I was left standing in the middle of the dance floor feeling sorry for this girl I didn't even know. As she wiped the blood from the corner of her mouth, I kneeled down to see if she was ok.

"Get away from me!" she yelled with tears in her eyes.

I could have verily easily given her a piece of my mind, but I figured she had had enough embarrassment for the night.

It didn't take Einstein to figure out the ball was over. I was now on a mission to find Clayton. I wanted him to enlighten me regarding the events that had just transpired.

Thirty minutes and two aching feet later, I gave up trying to find Clayton. I had searched the entire campus. It was obvious that he didn't want to be found. I decided to retire back to my dorm.

I had only been in my room for a few minutes before I heard a rock hit my window. There's only one person who throws rocks at my window. Clayton.

I looked out the window and saw him beckoning for me to come down. I had had enough drama for the night, so instead of getting all princessed down, I just threw on an old grey sweatsuit and headed downstairs.

"I just wanted to tell you face to face that I'm sorry about the way things went down tonight. I wanted the night to be special. But it looks like I messed it up for both of us."

He was looking so pitiful, I couldn't be mad at him.

"Look Clayton. I don't know what issues the two of you have. But whatever they are, you shouldn't have hit her."

"I know Daija. But you just don't know how she gets to me. She knows exactly what buttons to push and she's never satisfied until I_.

He stopped.

"Until you what, Clayton? Has this happened before? The hitting?"

"Let's just drop it ok. I'm not in a very sociable mood, so I don't want to talk about it. He had a nervous expression on his face.

"Look--I just wanted to tell you face to face that I'm sorry."

I kept having flashbacks of him hitting her.

"I accept. But I'm not the one you should be apologizing to."

"Friends?" he asked, as he extended his hand, obviously choosing to ignore my last statement.

Despite the dramatic events that had unfolded tonight, I couldn't help but smile at the puppy dog expression on his face.

"Yeah. We're friends till the end." I replied as I shook his hand.

He pulled me in closer and gave me a hug. Not the best night in the world. But I've had worse.

Chapter
Sixteen

"Elope?! Girl have you lost you mind?"

I could hardly believe my ears as I listened to the excitement in Angela's voice on the other end of the phone.

"Do your parents know?" I inquired.

"Don't worry. I got this under control. They think that we're not getting married until after Derrick and I both graduate. We're gonna keep this our little secret. And after I graduate, we'll go ahead with the wedding and all of that blah, blah, blah."

My burning curiosity made me blurt out the next question.

"You're not pregnant are you?"

"Heck no!! My parents would kill me." She laughed.

"Ahh, so you do care what your parents think." I facetiously pointed out.

"Of course. I've ALWAYS cared about what they think. Which is my reason for keeping the whole elopement thing a secret. I know my parents. And they would never go along with Derrick and I getting married before I graduate."

Angela had appointed me to be a witness at the marriage ceremony. Most people probably wouldn't be too thrilled to sit on greyhound for 48 hours, just to be a witness to a 10 minute ritual. I didn't mind though. Because not only did I want to see my best friend, I also wanted to see—first hand--what I had missed out on by not going to Howard.

After I got off of the phone with Angela, I sat down to catch the last few minutes of New York Undercover. Malik Yoba and Clayton could pass for twins. Maybe that's why I like the show so much. While watching Malik on TV, my mind started drifting off to Clayton land.

It has been over three weeks since the ball. He and I haven't really spent any time together since then. It almost seemed as if he was avoiding me. There were only five months of school left before graduation. And I have to admit that I missed his company.

Suddenly I had a bright idea.

Instead of riding the greyhound all the way to Washington by my lonesome, I could ask him to accompany me. The worst thing he could say is no. And if he said no, I wouldn't have reason to be embarrassed because he still doesn't know how I feel about him.

I pondered for a moment on whether or not I should walk down to his dormitory lobby and pay him a surprise visit. Then I decided not to because I didn't feel like taking a stroll down memory lane. I was in a good mood and wanted to keep it that way. I'll just make my way over to the band hall. Practice starts in an hour and I need spend some private time with my horn. Gotta keep my skills up to par.

Once I made it over to the band room, I pulled out my horn and started running through some scales.

As I was playing, some cold hands grabbed the back of my neck. When I turned around, I was shocked to see Clayton standing there. He was looking like a chocolate prince.

My heart started racing as I managed to put on a smile that hopefully didn't reveal the effect that his touch had on me.

"Hey. Where've you been?" I managed ask.

"I needed some time off. Had to sort through some things--ya know?" he stated with a peculiar nervous look on his face.

"Well. It's good to have you back. Ironically I was just thinking about you."

He looked surprised. "Good thoughts, I hope." he replied as he licked his lips.

If I didn't know better, I would think Clayton was flirting with me.

"I guess they are good thoughts. It depends."

"On what?"

"On what your answer is." I had now gone into flirt mode myself.

Clayton looked puzzled.

"Angela called me today."

"She doing alright?" he asked.

"Yeah--she's fine. As a matter of fact, she's getting married in a couple of weeks and wants me to come up to Washington to witness the marriage ceremony."

"You going?"

"Yeah. Greyhound."

"It's good that you're going. But the bus sucks. It'll take you three days to get to Washington on Greyhound."

He tried to change the subject. "So,"--clearing his throat--"what is this question that you have that'll determine whether or not you were thinking good thoughts about me?" His eyes were saying that I now had his undivided attention.

The conversation was heading in the right direction. With a little more twisting and turning, I would arrive at my destination. Which is to hear him saying that he would go with me to Washington.

"Well. Being that you are SUCH a good friend. I was wondering if you would like to grace me with your presence on my trip to Washington. If you don't, it will be a long and boring trip."

I was now waiting for a response.

His face had lit up like fireworks.

"You really want me to go with you? he asked as if he wasn't worthy.

I nodded my head in confirmation.

"But if you go, you can't tell anyone because it's a secret. She's eloping."

"Who am I gonna tell? I barely know her." He continued, "I gotta tell you though, I can't get down with greyhound. It puts a cramp in my style---know what I'm saying?" he stated, as he rubbed his conceited baldhead.

"So what are you suggesting?" I asked.

"I'll drive."

My heart was now leaping for joy. Those two words were music to my ears.

"I've been to Washington before. And there is a Hilton that's pretty close to Howard. I'll also go ahead and call to make us some reservations. I'll put a room for you and a room for me on my credit card."

I told him that we could just crash at Angela and Derrick's apartment. But he insisted on making reservations at the Hilton.

"You know they got auditions coming up for the U.S. Soul Symphony?" he asked.

"No!! Get outta here! Where did you hear that?" I shrilled in disbelief.

"It's posted everywhere on campus. I can't believe you didn't know that--ms. trombone prima donna. Why else do you think I gave up my hibernation to come over to this smelly old band room?" he smiled.

Clayton was pretty good on the drum. Perhaps the best at Valley. And unlike many others, he practiced his craft.

"If you wanna audition, you better go to the office and signup. Hopefully the deadline hasn't passed."

"Thanks. I'm on it." I replied as I laid down my horn and ran down the hall to the band office.

I was so excited as I headed down the hall. This was the best news I've had in a long time. The U.S. Soul Symphony is notoriously the number one Jazz symphony in the country. They play strictly jazz. And their full time job is to travel to and fro across the U.S. wowing the crowds with their unparalleled talents. If I ever became so lucky to make the cut, it would be a dream come true.

Turns out that today was the very last day to signup. There was one slot left. How weird and ironic is that? Maybe that's a sign. I signed my name on the list and picked up my audition material.

When I got back down to the practice room, Clayton had already started working on his audition piece. I didn't want to disturb him, so I sat back down and went to work on mine too. Auditions are in two months.

Mr. Davenport would be so proud of me right about now. And I wish I could talk to him to get some audition tips. But I didn't have any contact information for him. I haven't heard from him since right after Grandma Ginetta died. He would always tell me that it wasn't practice that made you perfect. He would say, "PERFECT practice makes perfect." And I know that if I want to be a part of the best symphony in the land, I am going to need a perfect and flawless audition. I closed my eyes and let Mr. Davenports words resonate over and over in my mind. I then starting reciting a scripture that Grandma Ginetta taught me at a very young age—"I can do all things through Christ who strengthens me...." After I had mustered up enough courage, I then opened my eyes and I practiced my audition materials as if my very being depended on it.

Chapter
Seventeen

We drove around Howard's campus for about an hour trying to find Angela's apartment. The campus was huge. There were student apartments spread out all over the place. And most of them looked alike, so it was hard to tell which was which.

We could have been there already if Clayton hadn't been too macho to stop and ask someone for directions. Apparently this is an issue with the male species that is still ungrasped by many.

Despite the fact that we were lost, the trip had been pretty good so far. Conversation was great. But, I still couldn't get him to tell me anything about Charlotte and what had happened at the ball. His response was simply "I don't wanna talk about it. Period." So I left that subject alone.

Unable to bear going around in circles any longer, I interjected the silence when I spotted a payphone. I had Clayton pull over so I could call Angela and get some sort of direction.

She was ecstatic when I told her that Clayton drove me up there.

"Where's he gonna stay?" she asked.

"He's already booked us two rooms at the Hilton." I bragged. "He insisted."

"Girl, I'm scared of you." she teased.

If there is any such thing as blushing through the phone--I was now doing it.

"Girl, I gotta go. I got the directions, so we'll see you in about thirty minutes." I slammed down the phone and turned to head back towards the car.

I turned so quickly that I caught him staring. He tried to play it off and looked in another direction. But I think he realized that he was busted.

Finally we made it to the right complex.

Clayton sat in the car, while I ran up the steps and pressed the buzzer for the speaker. They had one of those fancy apartments that won't let you get into the building unless you key in a code.

"May I help you?" a ladies voiced asked over the speaker.

I told her my name and who I was here there to see.

"One moment. I'll page Ms. Smith and let her know she has a guest."

Valley didn't have any apartments. And even if we did, they wouldn't be fancy like this.

When Angela came down, she appeared equally as happy to see Clayton as she was to see me. She gave both of us a hug and invited us inside.

"Will you look at the size of that rock?" I gasped as she grabbed my hand to pull me into the building. Clayton was right behind us.

"If this is the engagement ring, we're gonna need sunglasses for the ceremony tomorrow. The wedding rings are gonna blind us. Whatcha think Clayton?"

We both turned to look at him as I held Angela's hand out for him to catch a glimpse of her ring.

"No need for glasses. Since ol' boy is a doctor and all-- he can hook us up if we get blinded." he joked.

"Y'all crazy," Angela stated, "but he won't be able to fix your eyes, because he's not THAT kind of doctor. He's an ob-gyn."

"So when do we get to see this bridegroom?" I asked, trying to change the subject before Clayton cracked an ob-gyn joke.

"Yeah--good question." Clayton added.

"Actually, he's at the hospital right now. But if y'all ready to roll, we can go on over there to see him. I told him that we would more than likely be stopping by. So he's expecting us."

Angela took us inside long enough to show us their apartment. It was beautiful. The whole place was white and cream. White carpet. White walls. Off white leather furniture. The only thing that wasn't white or a shade of white, were all of the pretty colorful pictures that embellished the walls. They even had a white marbled fireplace with specks of grey. And a white marbled wet-bar.

I was so proud of Angela and how well she was doing that tears came to my eyes. I think part of those tears were also tied to me wishing that I was doing as well as she was. Wishing that I could find the happiness that she had found. I wasn't the least bit jealous. I just wished for a moment that things hadn't turned out for me like they had turned out.

"You ok?" Angela asked.

"Yeah. I'm just so proud of you that it caused me to get a little blurry eyed--that's all. But I'm fine."

"Alright. Let me go grab my jacket and we can get out of here."

Angela was gonna drive her car. But Clayton decided that he would drive so he could learn the city. We all hopped into the car and headed to the hospital.

It was huge. Had to have occupied every bit of ten city blocks. Johns Hopkins Hospital. The same hospital that treats the president—so it's deemed real prestigious.

Clayton and I sat in the lobby while Angela went to the ob-gyn station to have Derrick paged. A few minutes later, she came back grinning from ear to ear with a model looking brother by her side. I knew from the pictures that I had seen of Derrick that it was him.

He was handsome in the pictures. But in person, he looked like something that just stepped out of a Shemar Moore magazine. He had grown a mustache and a goatee. Which is something that he didn't have in his pictures. It made him look more manly.

Angela was giving me that "so what do you think" look.

"Angela and Clayton, this is my fiancé Derrick. Derrick, this is my best friend Angela and her boyfriend Clayton." she smiled.

If looks could kill, Angela would be SO dead right about now.

Derrick extended his hand to Clayton. Then to me. "Actually, he's not my boyfriend. We're just friends." I tried to laugh it off.

"You guys could have fooled me. He stated with a bassy voice."

Silence.

"So. Angela's told me a lot about you. You two use to be partners in crime. Or something like that?" he motioned with his hands.

"Yeah. Something like that." I winked.

Clayton and Derrick struck up their own little conversation while I pulled Angela over to the side bar.

"Girl! What was that?!

"What?" she asked with an evil grin on her face.

"Payback is something else." I pointed out.

"Whatever. So what. I had a little slip of the tongue. Don't even act like you didn't like the sound of those words. She started speaking slowly, "Angela and her BOYFRIEND Clayton."

"It did have a nice ring to it---didn't it," I laughed as we gave each other a high five and went on back over to Clayton and Derrick.

"Look, I hate to be brief," Derrick stated, "but I have to be heading back to work. I'm delivering my first baby." he bragged.

"You mean to tell me, you're suppose to be delivering a baby and you're out here talking to us?" I raised my eyebrow with a look of concern.

He laughed. "Naah. It's not like that. The mother hasn't dilated enough yet. So I'm just checking in on her every few minutes or so."

He kissed Angela on the cheek, "Nice meeting y'all. I gotta run. Angela's making dinner reservations for us tonight at La Bouche, so I'll see y'all there."

"OK. Nice meeting you too," Clayton and I said almost in unison.

After Derrick left, Angela took us on a tour of Howard's campus. It was like a beautiful city within a city. The tour was just another confirmation of what I had missed out on.

We eventually dropped Angela off so she could start getting ready for our dinner date. We then went to the Hilton so we could get ready and freshen up.

Chapter Eighteen

I hung out in the background while Clayton handled his business at the concierge.

He started getting a little loud with the hostess at the desk. And knowing how Clayton can get when he gets upset, I took it upon myself to intervene.

"What's wrong?"

"Nothing except ol' girl can't find the reservation I made for your room."

"Well, it's no biggie. Just get me another room."

"There aren't any more. They're booked."

"Cool. I'll just stay with Angela. It'll be like old times."

For some reason. Clayton didn't look to excited about the idea of me kicking it at Angela's apartment.

"You don't want to intrude on her and Derrick. They're getting married tomorrow. Don't you think they want some quiet time together?"

He did have a point. But I didn't let him know it.

"OK. So if I don't have a room. And the hotel is booked. Where else am I gonna stay if I don't stay with Angela?" I was starting to get a little agitated.

He turned his mouth up like Arnold on Different Strokes, "What you talking about Daija?"

"I'm serious, Clayton."

"Don't worry. The room that I reserved for myself has two beds. So you can stay with me."

"Why did you book a double occupancy room if you were the only one staying in it?"

"Who says I had planned on being the only one staying in it? he teased. I might have some honey's up here in Washington that was gonna come visit."

He was so full of himself. And talked more noise than a lil bit. But he had the looks to back it up.

"I'm just kidding." he confessed. "All they had were double occupancy rooms so I didn't have much of a choice. But hey, it worked out for the best. Right?"

He was so sure that I was gonna stay in the room with him. All I could think about was what happened when I was in the room with Judge. The rape. Some feelings came up that I hadn't felt in a long time. Feelings that I had tried so hard to bury and forget.

"Right?" he asked again awaiting a response.

"No. I can't."

"What do you mean you can't?" he asked. "I was a good enough friend to drive you all the way up here to Washington. So pardon me if I don't understand or if I am a little offended by your selfish response. I could have just said , "I CAN'T" when you asked me to come up here with you. But I didn't, because you asked me to."

Clayton had never talked to me like that before. I could detect a little hostility in his voice. Maybe he was right. We have been friends all this time. He's never come at me incorrectly. He's been nothing but a gentleman. So surely he wouldn't do anything like Judge did.

"Fine. I'll stay. But you make sure you stay on your side of the room." I gave a nervous smile.

"Where else would I be?" He looked hurt by my comment.

And if I didn't know Clayton like I do, I probably would have thought for a second there that he was honestly hurt.

After Clayton had finished checking us in, we proceeded to our room to freshen up for dinner.

I claimed my side of the room and turned on the TV so that I could listen to music videos as I ironed my clothes.

Clayton headed straight for the shower. And within a few minutes, steam and the smell of soap had starting seeping under the cracks of the bathroom door into the room.

The thing that made me nervous was that the only thing separating me from seeing Clayton's nakedness was a thin wooden door. I started trembling at the thought of what if he comes out of there with no clothes on and tries to take advantage of me.

I mean--I'm way up here in Washington in a hotel with a naked man in the bathroom. All of the old fashioned morals that Grandma Ginetta had planted deep within me had come to surface. I was starting to feel really, really bad.

While I was standing there ironing and having mental conversations with myself, the bathroom door slowly started to creep open. Out walked Clayton, dripping wet, with nothing but a white towel wrapped around his waist.

I was so startled that I accidentally knocked the iron off on the floor. As I stooped down to pick it up, I noticed that I was shaking.

Apparently Clayton noticed too, because as he got nearer, he asked if I was ok.

"Yeah. I'm fine," I whispered, as I pushed my hair back behind my ears. "Just a little cold. That's all," I managed a fake smile.

"They do have heat in here you know." He then went and turned on the heater.

I left the iron plugged in for him. Then I got all of my clothes together and took them in the bathroom with me and locked the door. I sat down on the toilet and started crying. "God, I need help. Please make these feelings go away. I just can't take this anymore."

It took me a moment to calm down. I then stepped into the shower and let the hot water provide a temporary soothing to my soul.

After I got out of the shower, I made sure I had every button buttoned and every zipper zipped. When I came out of the bathroom, Clayton had already gotten dressed. Which was a relief in and of itself.

As I curled my hair, Clayton asked me to explain to him why I was so nervous. My response was that I didn't want to talk about it. He kept insisting that I talk about it anyway.

Before I knew it, I had snapped. "Look. The same reason you don't want to discuss you and Charlotte—is the same reason I don't want to discuss the things that are bothering me!"

Clayton looked as if I had just slapped him. There was a long gap of silence.

"Clayton. I'm sorry. I didn't mean to snap on you. It's just that I have a lot of stuff bottled up inside of me right now. Some things from my past that have absolutely nothing to do with you. And being in this hotel room with you brought those feelings back. Feelings that I thought were gone. But they're not. And I'm sorry." I was now in tears again.

I felt like an emotional wreck. I turned to look back in the mirror at my bloodshot eyes.

Clayton eased over and put his hands on my shoulder.

"It's alright Daija. I'm cool. But if you ever need anybody to talk to. Or whenever you wanna get this thing off your chest. I'm here for you. That's what friends are for. Right?"

As always, he managed to draw a smile out of me.

"Right. Thanks for being such a great friend." I stated as I wiped away the remaining tears.

By the time I finished curling my hair, it was 6:30. We had agreed to be back at Angela and Derrick's place by 7:15 for our dinner date, so we had to get moving.

When we arrived, we found Angela and Derrick dressed in coordinating maroon and white outfits looking like Will and Jada. They were so cute together.

We didn't really have time to sit down because our reservation was for 8:00. We all piled into Derrick's crimson jaguar and headed out.

La Bouche was the most elegant and expensive restaurant I have ever set foot in. The cheapest entree was thirty bucks. And that didn't even include sides, salad, or sodas.

Because Derrick was treating, I just ordered a strip steak with a side salad and a drink. Despite my modesty, it was still right at fifty dollars.

Over dinner, Derrick told us a lot about himself and his family. His mother and father were both doctors.

Angela's face was all smiles as Derrick talked about himself. It's like his joy was her joy. His delight was her delight. The epitome of a happy couple.

"So what's your major Daija?" Derrick inquired.

"Music."

"What are you going to do with a degree in music?" he asked with genuine interest in his voice.

"Well. Actually, I have double major in music education and music performance. So if I don't teach, I'll be performing."

On that note, I informed Angela about the upcoming auditions for the US Soul Symphony.

"Daija, that's great! When are the auditions?"

"A month and a half from now. I'm so excited I don't know what to do. That would be like a dream come true for me."

"Yeah. I've heard them before," Derrick added, "they're pretty good."

"Clayton's auditioning too. So y'all wish us the best."

Derrick then started questioning Clayton about his major etc… While they were talking, Angela kicked my foot under the table to get my attention.

"Are you ok?" I read her lips.

Angela has always known when something was bothering me. I nodded my head and pursed my lips to let her know that I was alright, but she wasn't buying it.

"Y'all excuse me," she stated as she stood up, "I have to run to the ladies room. Daija--you care to join me?" she was motioning with her head for me to come with her.

"Yeah. I have to go too." I stood up and slid my chair back under the table.

"Women." Derrick teased.

"Tell me about it." Clayton agreed.

When we got in the ladies room, Angela sat down on the black leather sofa. She patted the sofa for me to come sit down beside her.

I slowly dragged my feet like a little child in trouble, as I walked over and joined her on the sofa.

"I may be hundreds of miles away from you. But I still know my best friend. I know things about you that you don't even know about yourself. For example--I know that you purse your lips when you're trying to hold something back. Just like you did when I asked you if something was bothering you. So talk to me. What is it?"

I could feel the tears starting to form in my eyes.

"I can't talk about it." I broke eye contact with her and found a spot to stare at on the floor.

"Daija. Talk to me." She reached over and rubbed my back to console me.

"You've been acting really weird every since our phone conversation right before I came to visit you for homecoming. I want to know what's wrong with my best friend."

"Angela. I didn't come way up here to rain on your parade. We need to be out there celebrating with your husband to be. Not in here worrying about me and my stupid problems."

"That's not important right now. I want to know what's bothering you. And we're not leaving out of here until you come clean with me. So start talking." She sat back on the sofa and folded her arms across her chest as she stared and waited for me to break the silence.

Uncle Willie and Aunt Tee-ona kept flashing through my mind along with scenes of Judge raping me. I kept hearing their voices reminding me to keep quiet about everything. I didn't want to hurt them. Didn't want to damage their reputation. But the pain that is rooted deep inside of me is unbearable. I can't keep it bottled up any longer. Before I knew it, I had started telling Angela everything. Everything that had happened to me. From the suicide attempt to the reasons I didn't tell anyone about what happened. We cried together for a while.   Then Angela took my hands in hers and said a prayer:

"Father God. Thank you for blessing Daija to still be alive and sitting in this room holding hands with me tonight as we come before your throne of grace and mercy.

Father, you know the hurt, the pain, and the guilt that she is feeling right now.   It's a pain that only you can heal. We ask that you dry up those emotional wounds right now Lord, in the name of Jesus.

We thank You for blessing her to have the Angels watching over her. Thank you for sending your messenger in the cafeteria that day Lord to let her know that you are an all seeing and an all knowing God.

Thank you for being her mother. Thank you for being her father. Her caretaker.

Thank you for being her strength when she is weak Father. We know that it was only you who brought her this far Lord. And we know that you didn't bring her this far to leave her.

Thank you Father for your word. You said that no weapon formed against her shall prosper. You are the supreme judge Father. Ruler of all.   We pray that you will bring her enemies to justice Father. And bless her with a peace that surpasses all understanding.

Thank you for taking care of her when she couldn't take care of herself Lord. Let her know that no matter what she is feeling right now Lord you are her Rock in a hard place.

Let her know that this battle is not hers. It's yours. We know you cannot and will not fail Father, in the name of Jesus.   Watch over her, protect her, and bless her in the name of Jesus. Amen."

After Angela finished praying, It seemed as if instantly the burden of holding it all inside was lifted. We took a couple more minutes to regain our composure before leaving out of the ladies room to rejoin Clayton and Derrick.

Clayton didn't even bother to ask what took so long. I think he knew that whatever was ailing me, I had been in the ladies room talking to Angela about it.

We finished dinner and went back to Angela and Derrick's place for a few hours before we headed back to the hotel.

When we got back to the hotel, apparently Clayton noticed my change in spirit.

He told me that he knew that I had talked to Angela. And just like Angela was my best friend, he said I was also his best friend and he was now ready to talk to someone about him and Charlotte.

He told me everything. I was in utter disbelief. He admitted that they had a violent relationship. He had been physically abusive to her for a long time. She was pregnant with his child. And he was mad at her for getting pregnant.

He broke up with her right before the pink ice ball because she was showing and he didn't want anyone to know that he had a baby on the way. She knew that. And that was why she showed up at the ball.

He admitted that he needed help with his temper.

The only thing I could tell him was to pray about it. I recommended that he go to some sort of counseling for his anger. He agreed that he would.

We sat up and talked until the wee hours of the morning. Talking about life. Things that happen in life. I went to sleep in peace. Some of the most peaceful sleep I've had in a long long time. And I wasn't even worried about Clayton being in the room anymore.

I knew there would never be anything between us because of the confession that he made to me on tonight.

I thanked God for closing the door on this relationship. Because it was a door that could have caused me tremendous pain.

This has been a very enlightening trip. And I am glad the both of us came.

Chapter Nineteen

The last few months of school were unbelievably pleasant. I was on cloud nine. Not only was I one of only five in the region to make the U.S. Soul Symphony, but Angela's mom had also assisted me in bringing Judge to justice.

When I came forward about the rape, it prompted two other girls to come forward as well. As a result, he was sentenced to twenty-five years in the county jail.

Of course, Uncle Willie and Aunt Tee-Ona weren't too thrilled. But I didn't care anymore. I had learned to stop putting the feelings of others ahead of my own just for the sake of keeping the peace.

Today, I have two graduations. As I sit here in my college graduation gown with all of my tassels that represent my various accomplishments and organizations that I have participated in, I am also wearing my spiritual graduation gown with the tassels that represent all of the hardship and pain that God has brought me through.

On my spiritual graduation hat, I had a NEW tassel of faith. Faith that God can heal all wounds. I have faith that no matter what happens from this point on, he is in control. Just as he has always been.

I couldn't help becoming overwhelmed with tears. These tears were unlike the other tears that I have cried so many times before. These were tears of joy. Tears of thanks. Tears of reflection.

After the ceremony is over, I will be boarding a plane and heading for Washington, D.C. to start a whole new life. A life of peace. A life of happiness. I'll be living out a dream that ten years ago I never would have imagined was possible.

I know it was only God who pulled me through. And today--right now--I just want to say thank you God, for being my Rock in a hard place.

To be continued.........

Printed in the United States
1436900001B/368